Angels Turn Their Backs

OTHER BOOKS BY MARGARET BUFFIE

Angels Turn Their Backs

Margaret Buffie

KIDS CAN PRESS

First U.S. edition 1999

Kids Can Press acknowledges the financial support of the Ontario Arts Council, the Canada Council
for the Arts and the Government of Canada, through the BPIDP, for our publishing activity.

Published in Canada by
Kids Can Press Ltd.
29 Birch Avenue
Toronto, ON M4V 1E2

Published in the U.S. by
Kids Can Press Ltd.
2250 Military Road
Tonawanda, NY 14150

www.kidscanpress.com

Edited by Charis Wahl
Designed by Tom Dart/First Folio Resource Group, Inc.
Printed and bound in Canada.

CM 98 0 9 8 7 6 5 4 3 2 1
CM PA 98 0 9 8 7 6 5 4 3 2 1

National Library of Canada Cataloguing in Publication Data

Buffie, Margaret
 Angels turn their backs

ISBN 1-55337-098-8

I. Title.

PS8553.U453A8 2001   jC813'.54   C98-930343-8
PZ7.B84An 2001

Kids Can Press is a Nelvana company

… an angel has no armor
Now torn and bent, no wings unfurl
We are looking for it
Oh we are looking for it now
We are looking for it
We need to find but one thing good

The world is big, the world is bad
But I will find the beauty – I see a vision in
My head – I am looking for it
Oh I am looking for it

Oh I am looking for myself
I am looking for it – I am looking for it now
I am looking for it
Oh I am looking for it now
Oh I am looking for myself

Looking for It (Finding Heaven)
Jann Arden, 1994

For Christine

PANIC

Close your eyes. Now think about the one thing that really scares you – I mean *really* scares the hell out of you. A spider crawling up your leg? Standing on a high ledge that's slowly crumbling under your feet? Maybe it's the fear of finding yourself deep deep under water, not knowing which way is up? Your lungs are bursting – you can't find the surface. Do you feel your heart pounding? Can't breathe? Is there a hard tightening in your chest?

Multiply those feelings by ten thousand. That's a panic attack. It's white light in your eyes. It's a bomb going off in your chest. And it's not being able to tell a single soul what's happening to you. You don't even know why it's happening. It's as if you've lost the *real* you and you don't know how to find her.

Now imagine having that feeling dozens of times a day. You're almost normal for a while and then, just when you're letting your guard down – beginning to relax – it shatters in your head.

How small a space can you hide away in? How small? How secret?

I was about to find out.

CHAPTER ONE

When a person finally admits to herself that she's crazy, what does she do next? March herself off to a nuthouse and turn herself in to a bunch of strangers who'll lock her up and throw away the key?

I don't think so.

I suppose if she has a best friend … but I didn't have a best friend.

Not anymore.

Some people might think I could just sit my parents down and tell them.

Not possible.

My dad was living a thousand miles away, full of self-satisfied "I told you so's." As for my mother, how could I tell a woman who's never afraid of anything that I couldn't go back to school that October morning because I was scared. Afraid to leave the house, afraid to walk two blocks – and even *more* afraid of walking into the place. She wouldn't get it. How could she? I didn't *get it* myself.

I really did try to go to school that day. I opened the front door. But then I just … stood there … unable to move. Black clouds of terror rumbled around, swarming me from all sides. I couldn't breathe, couldn't move. Ordinary people walked past the end of that ordinary walkway, on that ordinary wet October day. But if I walked down that sidewalk I knew I would die. Unless I could get back inside the house, the terror would shatter me into little bits all over that ordinary world. *Out There.*

When a car honked loudly and roared past, black dots bounced in front of my eyes. My feet stumbled back into the house, and the front door closed with a thunderclap that galvanized me up the stairs.

I'd left our second-floor apartment unlocked, just in case. I could hardly turn the door handle, my hands were so damp and flabby with fear. But now that safety was close, the darkness *was* receding a little.

I'd barely stepped into the flat when I realized I'd dropped my little shoulder purse at the front door – *and* the letter I was going to mail to my ex-friend, Jodie Markweel. What if someone found it and read the terrible things I'd written to her?

I hated being this wobbling mass of fear. What was wrong with me? I slid through the door and stood in the hall.

A sudden noise made the whimpering in my head go silent. There it was again – a kind of croaky chuckle that echoed through the locked door across the hall. When Mom had tried to include the room in our lease, our landlord, Harmon Wenzer, told her it was filled with the previous owner's stuff and he couldn't let us use it until he'd figured out what to do with it all.

I'd tried to tell Mom I'd heard someone talking and making weird noises behind that door, but she'd just laughed and said it was Harmon Wenzer and his friends in the flat below. I'd been forced to accept her explanation – until this very second.

The croaking noise was followed by a rattling sound, like metal against metal, followed by a loud hiss and another satisfied chuckle. Someone had to be standing right behind the heavily varnished door. Suddenly loud thumps sounded down the stairs beside me. I slowly peered around the corner railing, my hair shivering across my scalp.

No one was on the stairs.

A rush of cold air swooshed past my face, and I skittered backward into the apartment, dragged the chain across, and shot the safety bolt. I breathed for the first time in ten minutes but it was only a shallow skim of air. Tiny lights flashed and danced around me. I was going to faint. I *really was* going to faint, like some delicate Victorian maiden.

I stumbled toward my room and fell on the narrow bed. The ceiling shifted and lurched. I squeezed my eyes shut but I could feel the bed drifting under me. Good thing I hadn't eaten any breakfast, or it would be lying on the pillow.

I pulled Biddy, my old pink bunny, toward me and howled into her soft warmth. Crying always gave me a headache, swollen eyes and a sore throat. But sometimes it helped ease the fear a bit. For a while. It would come back and slash at me later on, but by then it would be more like a hiccup of what I'd felt at the front door.

When I pried my sticky eyes open, the ceiling was steady. I glanced at my watch. Nine o'clock. The memory of the school bell's shrill ring echoed through my head, and a band of anxiety tightened around my chest.

Deep breath. Keep it down.

What was I going to do? Mom would be beyond angry when she found out I hadn't gone to my appointment with the school counselor. That appointment was in twenty minutes. If I could make it, it would solve everything. Mom would be happy. The counselor would be happy. I wouldn't be happy – I knew I'd *never* be happy ever again – but that wouldn't matter. As long as I did it.

But I couldn't. I'd never be able to do it. Not Out There.

The dim light in the room made everything washed out, almost colorless. Small gray birds flew across the pale sky like shadows. It had been drizzling for days. The yellowing leaves of the oak that usually tapped against the window hung down, sodden and limp. Even though my face was hot, I shivered in the cold damp that seeped through the old house.

I paced back and forth in the little space between my dresser and the bed, trying not to wring my hands like an overwrought movie actress. I needed a good excuse to tell Mom. But what? It was no use. I'd reached the end of the road as far as she was concerned.

Chapter Two

The whole nightmare had started a month earlier, on the first day of classes. My new school had been teeming with kids – bumping, shoving, shouting, laughing kids. I'd stumbled up and down corridors feeling sick with anxiety. Part of me was angry, too. What was I doing here? I should be laughing and cracking jokes with Jodie at my old school in Toronto, not facing these screeching strangers.

At five to nine, I stood in front of my assigned locker trying desperately to open the combination lock that the hair-on-end school secretary had assigned me. I hadn't had the nerve to ask where the locker was located and I'd got turned around – going down the same wrong hallways again and again – until just by chance I'd found it.

I had no idea where my first classroom was, and the bell was about to ring any second. It was getting hard to breathe. The hallway seemed full of hot, dry dust. Right 26, left 0, right 6 – no, that wasn't it. I could barely see the spinning numbers as they jiggled in my damp fingers.

Someone shouted, "Whaddya think you're doin'? This isn't your locker, idiot, it's mine, so bugger off!"

A boy pushed his long pale face into mine. When he began to bang the side of his fist against the metal door beside my head, my heart pounded so hard I was sure it was going to break through my chest. I wanted to slug him right in his shiny braces, but my stomach was trying to force its way up my windpipe. Oh god, I was going to throw up!

Before I could move, the boy shoved me aside and I was caught up and spun around by a whirlwind of girls with voices so shrill I knew my brain was about to crack open.

That's when I dropped my books and ran. And I hadn't been back since.

I sat down on the bed and squeezed my hands between my knees. The Fear stretched its claws, its rough tongue licking at the edges of my mind.

"Go away, go away," I begged, but I couldn't hold back the images – my frenzied flight from the school, my desperate scramble over the railing behind the teachers' parking lot, the loud ripping sound when my new jacket caught on a nail. Even the sounds around me had altered, the honking of cars and the roar of buses on the busy streets sounding hollow and muffled, as if I'd been plunged under water.

I'd yanked open the small metal gate, run up the walkway, and banged through the front door, sobbing like a little kid.

"Hey, hey! What's up?" a deep voice had asked.

A huge figure wearing a leather apron and goggles stood in an open doorway – holding a metal torch. I think I yelped out loud before tearing up the stairs.

A few minutes after I'd reached safety, Harmon Wenzer followed me. I peered at him through the peephole in the apartment door. He filled the hallway: massive body, broad bald head, wedge-shaped goatee and all those metal studs bristling in his ears.

"What do you want?" I'd squeaked.

His deep voice called back, "You okay there, kiddo? Just wanted to make sure you were all right." Then he turned and shouted, "Shut up, Victor. I can't hear myself think!"

Who was he shouting at? Victor who? "I don't feel well," I said shakily. "I – I can't open the door."

"And you shouldn't. Maybe you should call your mom at work. You looked pretty sick down there."

"I will. I'll call her right now."

"Right-o. Hey, listen. I'm making some cookies. Would you like a few? I'll knock and leave them outside the door."

Baking? In a leather apron and goggles? With a torch? An hysterical giggle bubbled up but I cut it off with my fingertips.

"No. I'm sick. I – I can't."

"Okey-dokey." His face loomed closer to the peephole. "Need anything? Hot-water bottle? Aspirin? Ginger ale?"

"I've got all of that stuff. I'm going to the phone now and I'm calling my mom." I tried to make my voice sound threatening, but it only sounded high and twitchy.

"I'm off then. Rap on the radiator if you need me, kiddo." I heard him crash down the stairs to his apartment.

No way was I going to call *him* for help. And it was

Mom's first day at work. If I phoned her office, I'd have to talk to some stranger and get him to find her. I hated talking to people I didn't know. Besides, I'd whined for weeks about having to go to a new school. She'd think I was just faking.

So I didn't call.

When Mom came home that night, she'd found me in bed, with a hot-water bottle at my feet and a thermometer in my mouth. She'd stood in my bedroom doorway, eyes wide in disbelief.

"What on earth happened, Addy? Harmon just asked me how you were feeling. I had no idea what he was talking about. I thought you'd been at school all day. Why didn't you call? What's wrong?"

She threw her jacket on the foot of the bed, then felt my forehead. All of the worry boiled inside me again and I started to blubber.

"Addy, honey!" She hugged me, then pressed her lips to my forehead – taking my temperature. She didn't trust me where thermometers were concerned.

"You are warm," she murmured. "Oh, Addy. And on your first day of school."

I wiped my eyes with the tissue she handed me. "It happened after you dropped me off. In the hall, right in front of my locker. I just felt so sick. Now my throat's sore."

"I'll make you some hot soup. You'll feel better in the morning."

But I hadn't. I'd felt dizzy and sweaty even walking to the bathroom. I'd stayed home the next day. And the next.

And the next. That first week I'd been convinced it was the flu – convinced that the panic and the heart pounding that swarmed through me were just symptoms that would eventually go away.

But they didn't.

And later there'd been stomach cramps, headaches and little swellings on my eyelids that Mom called sties and treated with chamomile tea bags.

As for the landlord, Harmon Wenzer, he wouldn't stay out of our business. Every evening when Mom got home, he'd carry up soups and cookies and weird bottles of stuff he called tonics. Then they'd talk in the kitchen. Sometimes for hours. About what, I had no idea and I didn't care.

By the beginning of the second week, the mild sore throat was still there and I'd developed a rusty little cough. My ribs were sticking out like slender curved pencils just under my skin. I could manage to get down Jell-O or ice cream and ginger-ale floats and a few suspicious nibbles of Wenzer's plain cookies, but real food – like mashed potatoes or meatloaf – swelled in my throat and refused to go down. Just the smell of anything boiled or fried made me sick to my stomach. If I did swallow a few mouthfuls, I instantly got cramps. But I didn't have a temperature. I know – I checked it a thousand times a day, praying it would go up so I could somehow prove to Mom that I had to stay in the apartment – that I was too sick to go Out There.

Every day Mom had peered earnestly down my throat with a flashlight and tried to convince me to go to a doctor.

"Please?" she'd beg.

"No," I'd say firmly. "It's just the flu."

It had to be, because I couldn't go — not Out There.

Sometimes in the quiet dark of my room, listening to the silent approach of night where nothing moved except the black fingers of the tree outside my window, I would ask myself — what if it wasn't the flu? What if it was something much worse — a tumor, a small gristled knot of madness that somehow *made* my brain afraid of school, of taking even *one* step out of the house. Could it also make me hear weird noises from the room across the hall? Twice that week I could have sworn I heard footsteps coming up the hall stairs. When I'd peered out the peephole, there'd been no one there.

I was crack-brained, gaga, let's face it … nuts. All those times I'd pretended to be sick so I could get out of something — and now I really *was* sick. Except *now* the fever was in my brain, not my body.

Served me right.

Each day when she got home, Mom kept saying over and over again, "I don't understand it. No flu should be going on this long." Then she'd look at me with suspicion. Was I acting? Or was I really sick?

Finally, she'd phoned a roving medical service called Docs on Wheels. I hated being prodded and poked by a strange doctor, but at least she'd come to the house. As she packed up her bag, she said, "Well, it looks like she may have picked up a nasty little flu bug, Mrs. Jarrick."

I could have hugged that woman.

She smiled down at me and said, "A few more days – a week at most – and you'll be fine."

"So it's nothing serious?" Mom asked.

"I'm sure it's not. She's a healthy young girl. Too thin, perhaps. But you say she's eating a bit. Addy, I want you to drink plenty of fluids, okay? Milkshakes, eggnog, stuff like that."

I nodded vigorously.

"But what about her schoolwork?" Mom asked. "Should I call the school?"

The doctor nodded. "I'll just write them a brief note – they'll send work home for her." She put her hand on Mom's arm. "Don't look so worried. She'll be fine."

When they left the room, I fell back on the couch pillows and sighed with relief.

Mom wasn't happy, but she did what the doctor said. The school sent stuff home right away. It was easy and took me only a couple of hours each morning. I spent the rest of the time watching my collection of old movies and reading all my favorite books.

Now and again I'd creep downstairs to check the mail. To avoid making any noise, I didn't wear shoes. The last thing I wanted to do was bump into the Jolly Bald Giant, Harmon Wenzer. I always left my door open and stuffed my earphones into my ears to block out those strange noises – from the room next door and on the stairs. But slinking past, music vibrating my eardrums, wasn't worth it anyway, because our cloth mailbag on the back of the door never coughed up anything from Jodie. She'd definitely forgotten me.

One day, when I was about to try for the last time, I heard the thump of boots on the stairs, even over the wail of Alanis Morissette. I looked through the peephole and was actually relieved when I saw Mr. Bald Universe standing in the hallway. He took out a big set of keys. Jeez, was he going to just let himself in? Before I could decide what to do, he turned and unlocked the door across the hall.

I pulled out my earphones and listened.

"Well, you ugly old thing, let's have a look at you," he said. As the door closed behind him, I was absolutely sure someone had answered.

Later that evening, when Mom tried to force more of his homemade soup on me, I pushed it away. "He goes into that room across from us and talks to someone. He's weird. You should stay away from him."

"Don't be silly, Addy. No one lives in that room. He's probably making sure it's not being damaged – maybe by damp. I know he's had trouble with squirrels getting in the house through the attic. He could be putting down poison or traps, I guess."

"How do you know he isn't poisoning us right now?" I'd asked, pointing at the piles of herbs, yucky lima beans and zucchini floating in the broth.

She sighed. "Give him a break, Addy. He –"

"Why should I? All he does is poke his nose in our lives. I wish he'd just butt out!" I shoved my chair back and stalked out of the kitchen.

CHAPTER THREE

A few days after the doctor's visit, Mom had come home later than usual – right near the end of *Breakfast at Tiffany's*. I love Audrey Hepburn. She's perfect. Breezy, slim, beautiful – pure class. I have fish-white skin and bony knees. Just watching her as Holly Golightly always made me feel good, and that day she'd lowered my stomach-churning anxiety for a while.

Mom clicked the off button – just at the final love scene.

"Hey! That's my favorite part! It's almost over."

Throwing her coat on the back of the couch, she sat down on the steamer trunk coffee table. "It can wait. Right now we have to talk. The guidance counselor left a message for me when I went to pick up your school-work. He says the teachers won't have time to do this much longer. He'd like to see you, Addy. Soon."

I stopped breathing but managed to choke out, "I – I can't. I still don't feel well. I'll get sick – I *can't* – the doctor even said –"

Mom leaned forward. "I'm not saying you have to go tomorrow, but I've made you an appointment."

"For … for when?"

"Next Friday. That gives you a week. Work out a plan with him – get back into things slowly. Maybe just going to French and math for the first while – something like that."

One week. Then no more excuses.

The phone rang. I knew right away who it was when Mom cupped her fingers around the mouthpiece and answered in monosyllables. "Oh. Hi. Fine. Yes. No. Yes." It was Dad. I clicked the film back on and stared at it without really seeing it. Mom knew I wouldn't talk to Dad. She'd tried halfheartedly a few times to get me to the phone since we'd arrived in Winnipeg, but I'd refused. This time I knew she wouldn't even try, because suddenly her voice came out in sharp staccato bursts.

"I *am* doing the best I can, Wally. And your *bloody* unhelpful advice from a thousand miles away does *not* make this any easier. She's much better. Yes … *much.* She's eating just fine … yes, I told you …" here she gave a big sigh, "… yes, Wally, a *real* doctor. She says it's nothing serious. Don't start, Wally … just *don't start* …" Then I heard a clatter and a hollow crash, and I knew she'd hung up on him.

With a forced smile, she said, "Dad sends his love. He's worried about you. You are better, aren't you, honey?"

I looked up innocently. "Huh? Sure. By next week I'll be fine … right now though … I'm still not … you know …"

I let my voice drift sadly through the room like Holly Golightly sometimes did.

Mom stood in front of the television set. "Yes, but you are better, aren't you? You'll be able to go to that appointment – and then for regular classes, right? If you don't pick up this week, Addy, I'll have to take you to another doctor downtown. Your father insists."

My guts clenched into a painful knot. I clicked the off button on the remote. The magic of Holly was gone.

"I don't need another doctor, Mom," I snapped. "I am *better*. But not quite … ready to go back yet."

She rubbed her cheeks with the palms of her hands. "At least sit outside in the backyard and get some fresh air every day, okay? I don't want you locked away in this stuffy old house."

"I'll sit in the garden every afternoon, when you're at work," I said, just to get that worried look out of her eyes.

"And you'll keep that appointment. I could go with you –"

"No. I'll go myself. I'll *go,*" I'd promised fervently.

The week had flown by. And now here I was – missing the appointment. My bedside clock and my watch both read nine thirty-five, officially past the nine-thirty deadline. Like Ingrid Bergman in *Joan of Arc,* at sundown I was going to be burned at the stake.

Should I phone the school? Make up a big lie? I'm sorry I can't make my appointment because … because my nose is growing, like Pinocchio's? Or how about the truth? I'm sorry I can't come in today because I'm afraid to walk down the stupid, frigging street.

"Forget the school from hell," I muttered between my teeth. "Think about something else. Something safe. Something sane."

Like what? Like plans for fixing up this puny space I'd been forced to move into? Mom told me I could have it any color I wanted. Yes. Think about paint cans and brushes and rollers – about wallpaper – think about green, think about wildflowers or pretty stripes. Think about getting better. Maybe I should paint everything purple. Or bubble-gum pink?

Maybe I should paint it all black. Including the window.

Mom was going to force me Out There. I couldn't cover up anything. No more excuses. No more discussion.

If only there could be no horrible mind-numbing fear of going Out There.

I walked quickly into the kitchen, poured myself a glass of cold water, and sipped it slowly. I always felt better in this small room. The walls were covered in badly fitted confetti-dotted wallpaper, and someone had painted the new plywood cupboards with a single smeary coat of canary yellow, but it was almost cheery compared to the rest of the dingy apartment. Above the sink was a window over-looking the small garden and crumbling garage, and beyond that a narrow back lane and another row of big old houses.

Smoke puffed out of tall brick chimneys and hung like gray cotton balls over weedy gardens and unpainted fences. I liked that view – rain or shine. It was homey and worn and safe. It seemed to draw the hot fear out of me.

But never quite enough to let me actually go Out There.

Three times during the week when the sun struggled out from behind gray clouds I'd crept outside to sit on one of the wooden lawn chairs beside the overgrown herb and vegetable garden, praying Harmon Wenzer didn't spot me. I felt like a prisoner who'd been locked away in the dark for years – pale and blinking in the searing bright light – but within a few seconds I'd scurried back up the wooden fire escape to our apartment.

When Mom had asked if I'd followed orders, I'd said yes. I wasn't really lying, I told myself. I *had* gone outside.

I shivered. My inner thermometer was definitely out of whack. Now I was damp and cold, the linoleum a slab of ice through my thin socks. I turned on the new electric heater Mom had bought a few days ago. It crackled and pinged, and a faint electric smell filled the room. Wenzer was renovating the house slowly – at least that's what he claimed – but right now all we had were water-filled metal radiators that released sad little breaths of lukewarm heat. As soon as I switched on that heater I knew I'd made the decision. I wasn't going anywhere.

I was safe for a few hours more.

The fear slid back into its cave and I slammed an imaginary trapdoor on top of it. Lots of time to think up a really good excuse for not keeping that appointment.

Yeah. Right. Who was I kidding? You have to do it, Addy

Jarrick. You have to tell her. Tell her what? That I'm going crazy? That I'm hearing things next door? That I think the landlord is holding a prisoner in the room across the hall – like Mr. Rochester hiding his crazy wife from Jane Eyre? Maybe I should just tell her that I can't ever go to that school again because everyone will stand around in the halls watching me go berserk!

Fear wasn't new to me. All my life I'd been afraid. I couldn't remember a day when I hadn't worried about *something*. I'd cried my first day of grade school – okay, my first *month* of grade school. As I grew older, I learned how to hide the fear – most people even thought I was funny and a bit smart-mouthed.

I tried everything to get out of going to school when I was a kid. Sometimes it worked. Sometimes it didn't. One morning when I was ten – I had read how everyone fussed over Beth when she got sick in *Little Women* – I ran the thermometer under hot water and then sorrowfully held it up for Mom so she'd exclaim, "Oh, Addy, you're too sick to go anywhere, sweetheart!"

Instead, she'd explained to me that no human could live if her temperature was a hundred and fifteen degrees and I had exactly five minutes to get dressed. I heard her telling Dad about it that night, and he'd laughed out loud.

Mom said that when I was a little kid I'd hide in the hall closet when a heavy truck rumbled down the street. And if she left my side for two seconds in a store, I would bring the roof down. For the longest time, I'd been afraid to go to sleep, in case I didn't wake up. Stupid, huh? After that I was afraid of becoming a grown-up. Try to explain *that* one. It came like all the others – out of nowhere.

So you see – you name it, I was afraid of it.

I'd even quit Brownies, because I was petrified to be left alone with a group of girls I didn't know. I'd told Mom that everyone was mean to me, so I'd quit. The next week, she'd demanded that Brown Owl tell her who the bullies were. Of course, Brown Owl had denied everything, and Mom had indignantly marched me out, full of lies and happy to be free.

There'd been lots of times like that – Mom believing my fibs – me smothered in guilt and relief. But when I *had* tried telling her a few times how I was afraid of something, she'd gently given me her mini-lecture on "How Everyone Is Afraid at One Time or Other but You Just Have to Go Out There and Do Things Anyway."

A lot of help that was.

So I'd stopped telling Mom when I was afraid. Not even a hint about how worried I was leaving Toronto and moving to Winnipeg. Here was Mom – high-school cheerleader, school president. Now an award-winning filmmaker. What had happened to my 'Go Out There and Do Things' genes? I think I inherited Dad's 'Just Wait – Something's Bound to Go Wrong' genes. He was sitting in Toronto right now, waiting for Mom to fail and go back home, begging forgiveness.

But *I* was the failure.

Looking out over the shivering gardens, I could feel the bass beat of Wenzer's stereo thumping through my feet. That's when I remembered my purse – and that letter to

Jodie. I had to get them before he found them. He was just the type to mail the darn letter before I'd even decided if I wanted Jodie to get it or not.

I pulled on my sneakers at the door and was about to open it when the phone rang. I had just put the receiver to my ear when I remembered the school counselor. But it wasn't him.

"Addy? Is that you? Addy? It's Dad."

I hung up.

I would never forgive him. Never. He'd chosen to stay in Toronto, and now Mom and I were in a strange city, in a grubby one-bedroom flat instead of the great house they'd planned on renting. Let him rot in his boring gray office.

I looked around the Macmillan Street living room with its secondhand furniture and half-filled bookshelves.

"*He's* stuck away in a miserable place? Huh! Look at me. Like father, like daughter," I said loudly.

The phone rang again. Should I just let it ring? Or answer and hang up? It always gave me a weird sort of rush when I did that.

"Addy? Don't hang up. Don't –"

I slammed down the receiver and willed the phone to ring again, and when it didn't, I wanted to pick it up and throw it through the window.

CHAPTER FOUR

I ran down the stairs, anger following me like a swarm
of furious bees. I looked for my purse, but it wasn't
there. I glanced at the french doors that led into Wenzer's
apartment. Did he have it? My stomach squeezed tight.
Would I have to knock on Godzilla's door and actually
speak to him?

The front door opened and a girl walked in on a gust of
cold wet air, shaking a tattered umbrella.

"Wow! It's as cold and wet as a polar bear's ..." the girl
looked at me and laughed, a light tinkly little laugh, "...
nose."

She had a glistening cap of white-blond hair and dark
eyebrows that turned up at the ends like little wings.
The third-floor tenant. She and the guy she lived with were
hardly ever home, and when they were, they were either
arguing or playing loud music or laughing like hyenas.
Mom had gone up a few times to negotiate. She said it was
the girl who always came to the door, apologetic and
promising to keep down the noise.

"Winter's almost here," the girl continued, smiling at me.
"Soon we'll be up to *our* noses in cold wet stuff, huh?"

31

"Yeah, I guess," I said and gave her room to go up the stairs, but she didn't move.

"Hey, you live below me, right? Second floor? Harmon told me you've been sick for quite a while now. I hope you're feeling better."

I took a step back. Jeez, didn't anyone have any privacy when it came to that stupid Wenzer? All he did was poke his nose into my life. He lay in wait for Mom every evening when she got home. And now she talked about him all the time. 'Harmon told me if I needed extra work I could waitress at his pub.' 'Harmon says that summer savory is the secret ingredient in this vegetable soup.' 'Harmon's a well-known metal craftsman.' 'Harmon's half owner of a pub.' Harmon this and Harmon that. And now he was blabbing about me to perfect strangers – as if he *knew* me or something. I'd never eat one of his cookies again.

"Hey, you okay?" The girl smiled, showing slightly protruding teeth. "Man, you're really intense, eh?"

Why did people act like they'd instantly figured you out? It was so … *not true.*

A deep voice behind me said, "I thought I heard voices out here."

Harmon Wenzer stood in his doorway in black sweats and a plastic apron shaped like an enormous daisy. He had flour up to his elbows and looked like the strong man in a circus dressed up as some sort of twilight zone house-keeper.

"I – I gotta go –" I said, pointing up the stairs.

"I have your purse, kiddo," he said, "and a letter with your return address on it. I put it in the purse."

"Can I have them?" He'd called me kiddo again. That's what Dad called me.

"Hey, aren't you supposed to be at a meeting at school?" he asked.

How dare Mom tell him? I was really going to give her a piece of my mind. *But not before she gives you a big piece of hers,* a little voice inside me sneered. I couldn't even say I'd tried to go to school. Nosy old Wenzer knew I hadn't.

"Can I just have my purse?"

"It's in my kitchen. I'll get it."

The girl lifted her face and sniffed. "Mmm. Ginger and cinnamon. I only had one class this morning and it was cancelled, so I'm home to study. I didn't have time for breakfast … hint?"

His laugh was a deep rumble. "You're in luck. I finished that chandelier for All Saint's Church last night. Come on in. I've got the kettle on. First batch of celebratory ginger-snaps is just out of the oven."

"Sounds good."

He looked at me. "Join us?"

I shook my head. No way was I going in there.

"Okay. Just hang on and I'll get your purse."

I stood in the hall and waited. What was taking him so long? I was chewing on my thumbnail when I realized the girl was standing just inside his door, watching me with a faint smile.

"Coming in?"

I shook my head. "No. I gotta lot of homework to do."

"You still off school?"

"Yeah. For another week or so."

"So why not take a break?"

Why couldn't she leave me alone? "I – I can't."

"I'm Page Nesca, by the way. And you're Addy, right? Short for Adelaide, I bet?"

"It's not short for anything. Just Addy."

"You know, you should relax, Addy. We're not going to shove you in the cookie oven."

"I know that," I sneered, then flushed with embarrassment. "I mean –"

She took my hand and tugged. "Come on in. Visit."

"No. I can't. I've got to go –"

She put her other hand firmly against my back. I wanted to run upstairs – but I knew I'd look like a total idiot – so I let her drag me into Wenzer's place.

I was so surprised by what I saw that for a minute I forgot to be nervous. The main room was enormous, with big windows at the front and a set of three in an alcove on the side wall. Two orange leather chairs were arranged on either side of a glass and metal coffee table that stood in front of an old marble fireplace. A small fire was flickering in it.

The rest of the furniture was made of metal, including a number of chairs with mesh seats and a half dozen small tables with price tags attached lined up under the front window. Hanging from the ceiling were dozens of simple chandeliers. Dangling between them were wind chimes of all types. Shelves ran along the wall beside me, one section stuffed with strange clocks – big steel suns, moons and stars marked with curious symbols instead of numbers. There were also candlesticks, bowls and other objects I didn't recognize – all made of the same dull silver metal.

The corner with the alcove was clearly his work area. There were two big gray tanks with orange hoses attached to acetylene torches. Lying on the floor was a metal helmet with a glass panel in the front and a pair of leather gloves that would have covered my arms as well as my hands. Goggles of all sizes hung on hooks along with a couple of leather aprons. The whole alcove was covered with ceramic tiles, including a wide arc of floor, walls and ceiling. The rest of the floor was hardwood that glistened like burnt caramel.

"Sit down," Page ordered. "Harmon's cookies are worth it."

My sneakers seemed stuck to the shiny floor. I wanted to go home, yet, strangely, part of me wanted to stay too. Even though it was raining outside, the huge room was filled with light and warmth.

Harmon banged through the swinging door, my purse over his shoulder. "Sorry it took me so long. You can't leave these cookies past their time or they get overly crisp." He looked at me, surprised. "Good. You decided to come in for a bit. I'll just get the tea." And he disappeared again, taking my purse with him.

Page said, "Come on. Sit down, Addy."

I shook my head. My face ached from trying to look casual, but the girl was staring at me. To get her to stop, I perched on the arm of an orange chair.

"I gotta go … right away," I said, knowing it sounded utterly pathetic. "I need my purse and –"

"I know, I know, you've said that already. Relax," she said. "You gotta learn to chill, you know?"

She lowered herself gracefully to the floor in front of the small fire and drew up her legs, wrapping her arms around them. Then she leaned one cheek against her knees, looking at me out of the corner of her eye. I sat stiff as a plank, waiting for the rest of the lecture, but she just smiled and closed her eyes.

You gotta learn to chill. If only I could. She was so sure of herself. I could never be that casual, that … that *together*. I *never* sat on the floor – it seemed so phony, when there were perfectly comfortable chairs around. Mom's film friends did it all the time – drinking wine, talking in loud voices, not listening to one another. Trying to be so cool – even though they're really old. It made me cringe. The worst of them was Mom's old friend and new business partner, Sharon, who'd convinced her to take the job here.

"Call me Auntie Sharon," she'd insisted the moment we'd met. "Your mom and I may as well be sisters, right, Jill? That practically makes you my niece, Addy, eh?" And she'd given me a self-satisfied laugh, like someone snorkeling and talking at the same time.

Sharon would dump herself on the rug and talk and laugh louder than any of Mom's other friends. She didn't have kids, but that didn't stop her from giving Mom all sorts of advice about me. I absolutely refused to call her *Auntie*.

But this Page person looked as natural as a cat sitting in front of the fire. And her clothes were perfect. Tight black pants, short waist-hugging sweater, extra long sleeves that almost covered her hands, small scuffed ankle boots. White-blond hair with just the right amount of dark roots showing. Her long leather jacket lay over the back of the other chair. She had five gold studs in the ear facing me and a thin gold hoop through one nostril. And there I was, Fashion Addy, in my sweatshirt and jean overalls, grubby sneakers and single tattered braid down my back. Ugly.

The room was quiet except for the mellow tock-tock of the clock on the mantelpiece and the rain softly tapping against the windowpanes. When Harmon banged through the kitchen door with a loaded tea tray, he filled the whole space with a crackling energy.

"Here we are," he said, putting the tray down on the coffee table.

"You forgot my purse," I said, getting up. "And I gotta go."

"You're not staying?" he asked.

"Well, I –"

"Sit down and have a cup of tea, for pete's sake," he said, towering over me. I sat. "You be mother."

"Huh?"

"Pour the tea for us. Okay?" He smiled and his fierce face softened. He pushed aside Page's jacket and lowered himself onto the other leather chair with a grunt.

Trembling inside, I picked up the teapot and shakily poured three cups full, only splashing a bit when I set the heavy pot down again.

"Wake up, Page," he growled gently.

The girl stretched both arms high above her head. For just a fleeting moment, I thought I saw something flash above her wrist – a dark blue circle – but then it was gone. Page scrubbed her fingers through her pale hair and yawned before reaching to take a porcelain teacup from the tray. Her fingers were long, the nails short and uneven, as if she chewed them.

"So, here we are," Harmon said, popping a gingersnap into his mouth.

Page bit into one of the warm brown cookies. "Mmm. Positively ambrosial. Just what I needed."

I felt a twinge of anger. Like *she* needed anything. Jeez, she really was full of herself. I was determined not to eat, but Harmon held the plate under my nose, and for some reason I didn't want to hurt his feelings, so I took one.

He poured cream into my cup, dosed it with the full teaspoon of sugar I asked for and handed it to me. Tea sloshed onto the saucer. I'm pretty sure he saw how badly my hand was shaking and just pretended not to notice. I sat there, feet splayed, knees together, a cup in one hand

and a cookie in the other, unable to move.

Harmon began to quiz Page about school. It seemed
was in her first year at the University of Winnipeg. She
hardly looked old enough. And living on her own. I
frowned and concentrated on not spilling my tea.

Slowly the peaceful warmth of the room washed over
me. Not like our cold dark flat. Harmon Wenzer had
made this area his own special place – filled with all the
things he'd ever need or could possibly want. It surprised
me that someone who looked like the Incredible Hulk
could make a space that was so … peaceful. I wanted one,
too – somewhere that was specially mine.

I heard them talking in the distance, but I couldn't
seem to focus on what they were saying. It happened a lot
lately. I balanced my cup on the arm of the chair, leaned
back and closed my eyes. The sweet smell of the spicy
biscuit comforted me. Like when Mom used to bake on
Sundays. Now she didn't have time.

Time.

I'd run out of that. The long school hallway rose behind
my eyelids. I heard the boy's fist pounding on the metal
door and the screeches of the swarm of girls, saw the flash
of braces and the pink snarling mouth. I sat up with a jerk,
knowing my eyes had a wild, fearful look in them. I
quickly focused on the beige tea slopping over the rim of
the cup and jammed the cookie onto the saucer.

"… at your club tonight," I heard Page say. "Josh finally
talked your partner into letting us set up there. Thanks for

ck. "Bill called me about it. That's

. "Yeah well, Josh wants to have more
I've got so many assignments due. Now
he's ... out setting up gigs in Montreal and Toronto.
I'd like to ish the year here, you know?"

"You have to do what's right for you, Page," Harmon
said, "not what's right for someone else, or it ends up being
bad for everyone. I know it's a cliché, but it's true. Stand
on your own two feet. Be yourself. Do what's right for
you. Hey, sounds like a country song, eh?"

Do what's right for you, not what's right for someone
else? Did he actually believe that crap? Maybe this guy was
crazier than me. I suppose Dad believed it, though. Why
else would he have stayed in Toronto? If he had done
what was right for Mom and me, he'd be with us right
now. That little voice inside me sneered, *Yeah, and totally
utterly miserable.*

What *was* right for me? Going back to Toronto to live
with him? Oh sure. I couldn't even leave the house.
Hiding in the house and never leaving was right for me.
But how could I get Mom to understand?

"Addy? Hey! You okay, kiddo?"

My hand was shaking so hard the cup danced in the
saucer, and I had to hold it with both hands to lower it onto
the coffee table. "I – I gotta go," I mumbled. "I can get my
purse another time."

Harmon leaped to his feet. "Sorry, Addy, I'll get it right now." He rushed to the kitchen and returned with it and a plastic margarine container. He handed the container to Page. "Do me a favor. Feed that little devil upstairs, will you? Here's my key. Just leave it on the landing."

Harmon fed her boyfriend? It didn't matter. Nothing mattered except grabbing my purse and getting out of there.

Page took the container, threw her jacket over her arm, and smiled at me, yet I saw something sad and strangely familiar in her eyes. Before I could think of anything to say, she was gone.

CHAPTER FIVE

When the sound of her footsteps echoed up the stairs, I edged toward the open door. Harmon handed me the purse. "She's something else, huh? She and her boyfriend, Josh, have a band. She's the lead singer. Writes a lot of the songs, too."

"Yeah, well, that's nice." I slid closer to the door.

I was sure he could see the little muscle jumping in my cheek – how could he miss it? But he continued, oblivious.

"Josh calls the shots. He's –" he shook his head, "– but never mind all that. How are you feeling? You went white as paste there for a while."

"There's nothing wrong with me," I said defensively. "It's just that ... sometimes I can't ... never mind ..." I turned and stumbled out of the room. I couldn't even talk like a normal person.

I ran up the stairs but stopped dead on the landing. Page was unlocking the door across the hall. When she closed it behind her, I crept forward and listened hard.

"Take it easy. Man oh man, you are such a little pig!"

A voice, gravelly and shrill, squawked, "Shut up! Want more!"

Page laughed. "That's all you get. I'll see you later."

She was coming back to the door. I fumbled for my key, which I kept on a thick elastic wristband, but I was too late. The doorknob rattled behind me. I didn't want to talk to her again. I ran toward the stairs. Maybe I could hide out on the main floor until she went up to her apartment. But Harmon was crashing up the stairs two at a time, carrying a small plastic bag.

He said cheerfully, "Forgot these. He'd never let up without them. Having trouble getting into your place?"

"No. I – I …"

The door across the hall swung open. "Hey, what's up?"

"N-nothing," I stammered. "I was just going into my place –"

A disembodied voice screeched through the open door, "Who's here? She's here! Come on down. Come on down!" Then it changed to an imperious tone. "At once!"

Both Page and Harmon laughed.

"He knows we're talking to someone different," Harmon said. "You've been summoned into the king's presence."

"King? W-Who's he?" I asked.

Harmon swept the arm holding the plastic bag through the air in a medieval courtier's bow. "Please enter, dear lady, and we will introduce you."

I didn't know how to escape, so I cautiously followed him through the door. A dull gray light fell across everything inside the room like muffled dust. A big front window was covered with curtains and another facing the backyard had a closed venetian blind across it. A single pool of lamplight lit one corner of the room. There was enough light to see that the whole place was crammed with boxes, piles of paper-wrapped parcels and all kinds of other junk. A strange smell, like rotting apples, and something else – something I couldn't identify – filled the air.

Every hair on my body stood on end when suddenly from the illuminated corner of the room came a loud cackling, followed by fierce throaty mutterings of "She's here, she's here! Speak up. Speak up!"

Harmon laughed. "Addy, meet Victor. Neighbors were taking care of him for Lotta. When I bought the house and contents after she died, they figured he was mine, too. What could I do? I took him in, to my eternal regret. Isn't that right, you evil little sod? For months he didn't make a peep. Then, just a few weeks ago, he started croaking a bit, and now listen to him! He never shuts up."

An ancient voice snarled, "Where you been all my life, baaaby?"

"It – it's a bird!" I exclaimed. "A parrot!"

Harmon lowered his voice to a whisper. "I didn't tell your mom about him. I figured I'd find him a good home long before this. But he's not going anywhere, as far as I can see." Then loudly, "He can be a horrible child when nice people want to take him home. I had to drive one guy to emergency with a bitten finger. You're a pain in the butt, Psittaciformes."

"Pain in the butt, Harmon. Harmon Harmonica. Where's my sunflowers!" the ancient voice croaked.

Page giggled. "Isn't he a scream?"

I didn't think so. I thought he was scary. He was about eighteen inches tall and very shabby – patches of gray feathers missing all over his body and a red tail that looked like a comb with half its teeth missing.

"Scream, cream, we all scream for ice cream," the bird squawked.

Harmon snapped, "Shut up, Victor!"

A loud shriek of anger filled the room. "Will not!"

"Oh yes you will," said Harmon firmly. "You talk too much." He turned to me. "He's very lonely and very bored. That's why he's started plucking out his feathers. Poor old fella."

"Poor Victor. Poor poor Victor," croaked the bird, followed by a little sob.

"I thought parrots were yellow and green and blue," I said.

"Most of them are, but Victor's an African Gray." Harmon opened the bag in his hand and filled a tray with sunflower seeds. The bird eyed them suspiciously. "I can't have him in my place because of the fumes. And I can't sell him – can't even give him away. And Josh doesn't want anything to do with him, eh, Page?"

She shook her head. "We hear Victor through the air vent, making all sorts of weird noises. He gives Josh the creeps."

"Creepy Crawly Josh. Creepy crawlies. Poor little Victor Boy," the bird crooned into his sunflower seeds. "Poor little orphan Vic-toir. Please ... sir ... may I have mooore?"

"He can't really know what you're saying, can he?" I asked. "Why does he sound as if he does?"

"African Grays are extremely intelligent," Harmon said. "They're amazing talkers. So little Oliver Twisted here fits *the bill,* so to speak."

Page giggled. Harmon grinned at her. "I found some books about parrots in among the mess in the house when I bought it. One said some Grays have tested equal to primates in intelligence."

Page poked the cage. "That's what you are, Victor, a little *ape.*"

The bird answered with a series of giggles that sounded just like Page. Then he glared at me. He began to flap and run around his cage, up and over the bars, finally hanging upside down using his thick claws for balance. Small gray feathers floated in the air like light snow. He stared at me through them, banging his beak on his dish. Then he stretched his neck, picked out sunflower seeds, and sprayed them through the bars.

"Talk to me, baybeee! Talk! Talk!" he screeched.

"Can't you make him stop?" I cried, backing away from the noise.

Harmon grabbed a quilted dome-shaped cover off a hook and dropped it over the cage.

"He'll settle down now," he said.

Deep muffled mutterings could be heard from beneath the cloth cave.

"He can't really know what he's saying, can he?" I repeated.

"I don't know — but it's uncanny how often he matches his responses to the person speaking," Harmon said. "Mind you, Lotta probably talked to him all the time — sure didn't have anyone else to talk to. Never left this place. Not for many years, according to the neighbors. These birds cost big bucks, let me tell you. Probably a lot more than your scrawny ass is worth, Victor, old lad."

"Shut up ... you just tick a lock!" came a muffled growl.

Page giggled once again and Victor giggled back — a perfect echo. Very creepy.

"This Lotta owned the house before you?" I asked.

"Yeah. Her last name was Engel," Harmon said.

"Is this all her stuff?" I asked.

He nodded. "It was. I stored her furniture except for what's in here. I think she used this as a kind of sewing room. There's a lot of cloth and sewing things. I think she must have been a dressmaker or something. Many of these parcels and boxes haven't been labelled, but because they've been packaged so carefully, I assumed they were important to her and put them aside. Haven't had a chance to look at them."

Page asked, "So what will you do with all this junk? Josh thinks some of it might be valuable."

Harmon looked at her sharply before shrugging. "I doubt it. I think most of it is curtain or dress fabrics. She didn't get rid of much from what I can see. I keep meaning to have a good clear-out in here, but I never seem to find the time." He looked at me. "Hey, you wouldn't like a job, would you? We could put any interesting stuff in the basement until I can decide what to do with it. We can give the rest to the Salvation Army."

I looked around at the shadowy piles of boxes and bundles. "I don't know – I'm pretty busy."

Page laughed. "That's exactly what I told him when he asked me last month. I haven't any more time than he does. Hey, I bet Josh would –"

Harmon said quickly, "I think Lotta'd like a female touch on this. We'll forget it for now ... but I'd pay handsomely, Addy. Plus you and your mom would get an extra room. Look, I've gotta get to work. It's going to be a busy night at the bar. Page, when you leave, take off his cover and open the blind and curtains. I'll cover him again tonight when I get home. He's got lots of water and food, but a bit of company would be nice. And, Addy, tell your mom I'll expect her around eight o'clock."

Expect my mom? Before I could ask, he was out the door and thumping down the stairs.

CHAPTER SIX

"Eight o'clock? Sounds like a hot date to me," Page said with an impish smile.

"Well, it's not! My mother would never go *out* with someone like him. Besides she's married."

"But your parents are separated, right? And what's wrong with Harmon?" she asked. "I think he's cool. Your mom can go out for coffee – she's not a nun, right?"

Would Mom go out with him? She hadn't said anything about going anywhere tonight.

"My mother would have told me if –" I began, but she walked over and partially opened the heavy curtains over the front window, and I was immediately distracted. Smack in the middle of the room was an old dining-room table and chairs heaped high with junk – books, folded fabric, straw baskets overflowing with balls and skeins of wool, and teetering piles of cardboard boxes. There was hardly an inch of wall space in the little room that wasn't lined with shelves. Some of them held books but most had been divided into cubicles crowded with bolts of cloth, colored plastic containers, shoe boxes, spools of threads, and rolls of wool.

Against the window that faced the backyard stood a plain unvarnished worktable covered with sewing stuff – scissors and pincushions, a scattering of more little bundles of wool and silk, and heaped rolls of light brown and white fabric netting. I knew from my craft kits that this was needlework canvas.

To my right, tucked in the far corner, was a small white fireplace. One old armchair, loaded down with folded fabrics and books, sat at an angle to it in front of the window with the half-opened curtains. A standing lamp with a dark shade stood nearby. There was also an amazing number of paper-covered parcels piled onto dining-room chairs, shelves and small tables. Larger ones were stacked on the floor against the wall.

I walked over to the worktable. On a shelf just above it sat a large silver-framed black and white photo of three people – a young woman with straight shoulder-length black hair, short bangs and an angular unsmiling face; a teenage boy with a large round head and a big smile; and a younger girl with blond curly hair and a slight frown. I couldn't keep my eyes off the older girl.

"I wonder who this is," I muttered.

Page's voice was so close behind me I jumped. "I've looked at it. Their names are on the back. Lotta is one of them. I think the dark one."

I turned the photo over. Someone had written "Me, Eli and our little angel, Becca." She had written a name in the right-hand corner. *Lotta Engel*. Page was right, the dark-eyed intense girl was Lotta.

"Hey! She looks a lot like you," Page said.

I bristled. "I don't think so. Not a bit." I put the photo back on the shelf.

"No need to get worked up about it."

I glared. "I'm not worked up."

She glanced at her watch and let out a little squeak. "Yikes, I gotta go! Do me a favor? Open the blind and stay with Victor for a bit? I promised to phone Josh at the bar. He'll be … you know …" She shoved the key into my hand.

"Hey. I can't stay here – I've got to –"

She cut me off. "Please? Thanks a million. Talk to you later." And she was gone.

I was about to follow her when a muffled voice said, "Stay with meeee. Help me. Hot. Stuffled!"

I dragged the cover off Victor's cage, then stood back.

He leaned close to the bars and in a husky whisper said, "Nice girl. Stay?"

Shivers went down my arms. "I'm going to open the blind and then I am leaving," I said, trying to keep my voice firm.

He stiffened and fell off his perch. As I leaped forward to see if he was okay, he twisted his head up and croaked, "I die of aloneness. Stay. Please … stay …" and followed with a couple of pretty convincing death rattles.

A laugh burst out of me.

"Not so fun. So sad. All alone," he squawked, climbing onto his perch again.

"Okay, okay. But don't bug me. The minute you start screeching or acting weird, I'm out of here."

"Tick a lock," he muttered. "Viccky ticky lock." And he fell silent, his eyes riveted on me.

I grinned, realizing this was the first time I'd laughed out loud in weeks. It felt good. I put the key onto the little clip on my wristband, next to my apartment key, then wound my way through the piles of stuff.

What was in those parcels? I kneeled down beside one of the bigger ones and pulled on the simple string bow. Inside was a rolled needlepoint canvas with a design sewn on it – a repeated diamond pattern of flowers and exotic birds, including parrots. In the center diamond was a tiny figure wrapped in dark green material that floated out into the space surrounding it. Black and green feathered wings rose high above its shoulders. Its head was turned to the side, long white hair covering most of the face.

I picked up the next parcel and unwrapped it. This one was a close-up of a door, the bricks around it beautifully shaded in soft brown silks. A dark vine, studded with vicious-looking thorns and heavy drooping roses wound over the bricks. The door's knocker was another winged creature sewn in shades of deep gold that looked like shiny brass. The tiny figure was frowning down at a rose petal that had landed on one of its upturned hands.

I opened another and then another. There was an angel in every design, with large wings of different colors, from deep orange to bright fuchsia to dark blue. They were strange, curiously ominous figures – some with faces covered, some with fierce eyes and dark expressions, others with joyous smiles. They weren't like any angels I'd ever seen in books. They weren't fairies either, for their wings were the large feathery type that angels usually had. The only angels I remembered had sweet simpy faces and white feathery wings. These looked like real people – with human feelings – sadness, anger, humor. One tiny figure standing between the ears of a marmalade cat holding a pair of large cymbals – while the tabby watched a mouse creep out of its hole – had a look of downright wicked pleasure on her face. A title had been sewn into the design. It was called "Apedemus Guardian Angel." What did that mean?

What did they all mean?

Victor was rattling the cage and muttering to himself, but I was too preoccupied by the ring of magic and color and light that surrounded me to pay much attention. I'd worked on quite a few needlepoint designs over the past year, but they were nothing compared to these.

There were a number of floral pictures, too – large blowsy peonies and tall elegant gladioli, some in Victorian urns decorated with winged figures, and other designs where the angels were decked out in vines and blossoms. And there were animals too – a fat squirrel with a pale yellow angel; a frog sitting on a broad green lily pad with a vivid blue-winged creature sitting beside it; a heavy gray bulldog sprawled over a tasseled pink cushion, a tiny angel curled up asleep beside one of his thick paws – and another scene that vibrated with dragonflies hovering through large red leaves – a small chartreuse figure leading the way. The colors shimmered, glowed from within.

I knew I should pack the parcels up again, but I hated the thought of hiding them away. Harmon was wrong. This was no ordinary sewing room. Hadn't he been curious enough to look inside even one package? Probably not. Probably he was like Dad — only caring about his own work. His own miserable, selfish, self-centered life. My anger at Dad overwhelmed me suddenly and I had to walk around the room. That's when I noticed a pile of flat parcels on the dining-room table.

More designs? Another treasure trove? I peeled the paper off the top one. The framed design was of a night sky, glimmering dark green trees and distant purple fields — all created from silken threads. This wasn't needle-point, but true embroidery. A group of fabulously deco-rated angels hovered in the night sky, each one playing a different instrument. Fantastic.

The package beneath it was wrapped in black shiny cloth. A number of colored silk threads had been used to tie it shut. Suddenly I felt guilty. What was I doing tearing my way through someone else's stuff?

I heard a thin sigh right beside my ear and a cold finger of dread slid down my back. At the same time, Victor croaked, "Victor talk now?"

My knees were shaking but I had to laugh. "Yeah. Just so I don't think I'm going completely crazy hearing things."

"Don't you worry," said a deep, smooth voice. "Do what you have to do. Open it up. Go ahead. I'd like you ..." the voice changed back to Victor's scratchy squawk, "... to see it."

How could a bird speak so clearly ... and make so much sense at times? How could he know what I was doing, let alone thinking? I stared at him. He stared back. Then he lifted his head and cried, "She make me do it. Shut up, Victor! Talk, Victor. Tick a lock, Victor. Speak, Victor. I'm a good boy. Open it."

I looked at the black parcel in my hands.

"Open, open, open!" Victor chanted.

The colored threads and the silk fabric slid to the floor with a faint swish. Inside was a tapestry, about two and a half feet square. The entire design was five rectangles – one in each corner and a middle one that overlapped the others a bit.

Fascinated, I turned it toward the light. The middle square was filled with a wide-spreading tree, its branches full of all sorts of things – books, fruit, birds, animals, scissors, spools of thread – like tiny Christmas decorations. The roots of the tree were exposed and echoed the shape of the branches until they curved inward around a pale blue orb with shadowy shapes inside.

In each of the rectangles surrounding the tree was a different scene. The top left-hand corner was clearly this very house, only it was painted white and green. Five people stood in front of it – a boy, a tiny girl, an older girl with a deep red ribbon pulling back straight black hair, a man and a woman. The children looked like the ones from the photo. They were holding hands and smiling. The colors were bright and the pattern simple – like a child's painting. Above them, clouds scudded across the blue sky, with vibrantly colored grinning angels hanging on to them, their wings streaming out behind.

The top right rectangle had two figures. The girl with the red ribbon stood surrounded by books and toys and sewing baskets with spools of thread dancing around her head. Looking over her shoulder was a beautiful buff-gray and bright-red angel. The colors reminded me of Victor. Her guardian angel? The shading and artwork here were detailed and realistic.

In the lower left-hand rectangle, the girl looked much older, but I recognized the black hair and red ribbon. She was alone – hunched over in a chair, sewing on a piece of fabric. She looked sad, almost defeated. Although many of the colors were dark or muted, there was a strange reddish swirling sky just behind her left shoulder. On the piece of fabric she was sewing, I could make out the rounded shapes of four tiny gray squares, no not squares – I felt shivers go up my arms – four gravestones. In front of her was the dim shape of an angel's wing, a few blood-red feathers scattered around her feet.

In the final section, dense black clouds surrounded a shape like the arched window of a church. At first I thought it was a stained-glass window, but when I looked closer, I saw thin black bars running vertically over a figure hunched inside as if in a small prison cell. The sides of the "window" seemed to press in on the gray and red angel. Wings bent, head and shoulders down, one of its arms was stretched – palm out, as if trying to push its way out of an ever-diminishing space.

The unearthly glow of the ruby feathers was shocking against the darkness and the struggle inside the enclosed space. I felt as if I was being suffocated. I leaned away and sucked in a deep breath.

"Wow," I said. My chunky, awkward designs were full of dull, boring subjects – a little black Scottie with a plaid collar or a robin on a spiky, unnatural-looking branch. Nothing like this. Nothing that breathed and echoed with night sounds and secret whispers and ... pain and loneliness. I felt so sad for the girl. I knew how she felt. But who was she grieving for? The family in the picture above? I wrapped the black cloth loosely around the tapestry in case I wanted to look at it again.

Victor bobbed his head up and down, his sharp eyes glittering. In a silky voice, he said, "Stay here. I need your help."

That voice was spooky, as if a woman was right beside him, using him like a hand puppet. I was being silly. *Polly want a brain?*

I sat down on the edge of the dusty armchair in front of the cold fireplace, yet I felt cozy and warm in this small alcove – as if I'd found a secret spot that could be all mine.

I leaned back and closed my eyes.

"Lullabyeee and good niiiight," sang a throaty voice.

I sat up. "You're crazy!"

"Crazy is as crazy does!" came the reply. "Oops! Shut up, Victor!"

"It's okay, Victor," I said. "I know I'm crazy. But let's just keep it between us, okay?"

"I was crazy once. Everyone said so – sew a thread – close your mind – stitch it up – that's what they told me – stop the sights – don't listen – no one listened." The strange womanly voice coming out of Victor was tight, forced.

That did it. Better get out of here. I knew parrots mimicked, but this was plain creepy. I'd just grabbed a roll of plastic to cover the tapestries when I spotted something near the worktable. It was a wooden needlework stand covered with a piece of unbleached cotton. I'd asked Mom for a frame just like it for Christmas. Maybe Harmon would let me use this one for now. I lifted the white cloth off it, expecting to see an empty square, but there was a large piece of canvas attached to it with a partially finished winged creature floating alone in a dark sky, its back toward me. Its wings had a raggedy look, as if the angel was injured or had been given a pair of defective wings. Or maybe it was because only the outside rim and half the inside were stitched – the tips a deep sooty red – the other parts dull gray.

Barely half the background was covered in blue-black stitches, the rest naked canvas. Below the outline of the creature's bare feet was a wide band of plain unstitched fabric. What had Lotta intended to put there? My fingers ached to start sewing. But where – how would I begin? I traced my finger over it trying to decide, then quickly pushed my hand in my pocket.

How could I even think about touching it? This design, this room, they belonged to someone else, not me. And that someone was dead.

So what was it that made it feel so right?

"The angels turned their backs on you too …" Victor crooned in that weird "other" voice. "You belong here. Stay with me. Don't leave me alone. Not until it's done."

Suddenly, he crackled, "Use it. Use me. At your service. Service with a smile. Onnnly youuuu can make the day seem bright … only youuuu can make the darkness light …" Then he began to squawk, "You're wrong, silly bird! Shut up, Victor. No I won't! Bad Lotta!"

Was he arguing with that other voice? *Definitely* time to get out of here. As I inched toward the door, the cage seemed to loom closer, Victor sitting very still, head down, eyes locked on me. "You'd better come back. I'll be waiting."

My bones jumped inside my skin as if I'd touched a raw electric wire.

"You're crazier than I am!" I gasped, racing toward the door.

Victor screeched. "Hey, girl! You come back now, you hear?"

I had slammed the door and locked it when I heard a loud crash and then a series of sickening thumps on the stairs. I didn't stop to look. I didn't want to know. As soon as I was safely inside my apartment, I realized I'd left my purse behind. No way was I going back into that room. Not ever.

CHAPTER SEVEN

I ordered myself to calm down. Victor was just a dumb bird into noises, and I was all nerves and electric wires and sparks. I had to get a grip. A tiny hammer hit a nerve above my eyebrow over and over. I wandered into the living room, rubbing at it with the heel of my hand.

The rain had stopped. Everything outside was misty and edged in gray, the cars and trees along the boulevard standing like dark shadows ... waiting. For what? For me?

They'd have a long wait.

Below, Harmon's bald head and wide shoulders moved above the leaf-spattered front sidewalk. He'd changed into jeans and a leather bomber jacket. He turned and looked back at the house, then right up at me, and waved. How did he know I was watching him?

I waved back, feeling bereft and not quite real, and he walked away into the haze, like a ghost moving into cemetarial gloom. I'd felt like that for weeks now – not quite solid skin and bone. Would I soon fade away into nothingness? One day – poof! – no more Addy ... just a smudgy memory, like that faint grease spot on the wallpaper beside me?

Not much of a loss.

I could hear my mother, 'You've got to go out there and get to know people, Addy – get involved.' Yeah. Sure. Like today? I could hardly talk to Harmon. I'd almost enjoyed talking to Page in Victor's room, until she left me with the scary old thing. She was so lucky – going to university classes, having Definite Opinions on things, singing in a band, having her very own apartment. She was someone with a *life*. I pressed my forehead against the cold glass. I didn't have a life.

I was utterly pathetic.

I didn't even have one single friend. Someone like Page might be willing to talk to me, but she was older and what would she say if she knew I wasn't playing with a full deck anymore? More like fifty-two pick-up. All over the place, that was me.

You couldn't trust friends anyway, I'd discovered. My best friend was *someone else's* best friend now. I should have seen it coming. We couldn't have been more different – Jodie, red-haired and freckled, outgoing and friendly. Me, tall, scrawny, dark-haired – basically your Arch-nerd. Jodie could have been best buddies with anyone, even the popular girls, but she made it clear she really wanted to be *my* friend. When the other girls said rotten things to me, Jodie told them to shut their traps.

I'd told her dozens of time to ignore them, but once she'd even landed in the principal's office for "creating a scene" in the hallway, all because some girls had been teasing me. She'd walked back into class grinning and that had really impressed them. They'd seemed in awe of her.

Most of the girls had been just plain indifferent to me, but some of them – where did that awful hatred come from? I mean, it wasn't like I was a threat. My two front teeth overlapped, and I had long board-straight hair that always looked chewed off at the ends no matter how often I had it trimmed.

Jodie figured she knew. "You're okay looking – lots of hidden potential ... extremely hidden ... hah! ... but they're *really* jealous because you're – well – you're different, you know? You're just about the smartest kid in the school, maybe in the universe." And she'd nodded emphatically to let me know she was right.

Having brains was part of it, but deep in my heart I'd always known that the other girls were mad at me for being so ... separate. I'd rather read Amy Tan or Jane Austen than hang out with girls who giggled at everything some unbelievably dense boy said in class.

And they knew it.

Yet, when I found out we were moving to Winnipeg, I felt as if someone had hit me right over the heart with a baseball bat. But Mom and Dad were moving, so I had to go, too. Jodie and I had vowed to write each other every single week, and she'd promised to come out to No-Man's-Land and visit me next summer.

I'd kept my side of the bargain, writing her almost every day for the first few weeks, but Jodie'd only written once, a scribbled note that casually mentioned she was hanging around with Tiffany. Tiffany was one of Them –

the ones who'd called me names. I'd stared at the single page for a long time.

I had been betrayed.

That's when I knew it was better … easier … to be alone. No one can hurt you if you stick to yourself, right? So I'd written her the letter that was in my purse, telling her I didn't want to hear from her again. Only I hadn't said it quite that nicely. But why bother? It's not as if sending it would change things. There were Tiffanys everywhere – like the ones who'd pushed me aside and screamed in the hallway that day in the new school. Like the ones who stole away best friends. Like the ones who said they'd be true-blue and weren't.

We'd done everything together, Jodie and me.

I wiped the back of my hand across my damp nose and drew in a ragged sigh. A few people wrapped up in scarves and thick woolly hats walked by under my window. Most of them looked hunched and miserable. Like me.

But they were Out There. I wasn't. I was different.

Soon Mom would be walking up that cold, concrete path like the grand executioner. I had to be ready for her. Like Harmon said to Page, 'Do what's right for you, not what's right for someone else.' Staying home was right for me, I knew it was.

Harmon had also said, 'Be yourself.'

What did that mean? Was the real me the crazy one afraid to leave the house? The one who was afraid all the time? Was that the real me? It was like I was two people – each watching the other – not knowing how to make a complete, normal ... *me*.

Fatigue fell over me like a thick blanket. I needed to sleep, to wipe out these weird, flitting, unconnected thoughts. Too much thinking. Too much worrying.

As I was about to turn away from the window, a cab ground to a stop in front of the house. A boy hopped out of the back seat. He was tall and skinny, dressed in Army Surplus khaki. His hair, the color of the wet oak leaves, was short and brushed forward like an ancient Roman's. He hitched a backpack over one shoulder and a guitar case over the other, paid the cabby, then turned toward the house.

At the gate, he stopped and looked the place over. He stared straight up at me just as I stepped back into the shadows. I heard the distant echo of Harmon's doorbell. A few seconds later, the buzzer to my apartment echoed down the hall.

The shrill sound filled the apartment again and again. Who was he? Why didn't he go away? Couldn't he figure out that no one was going to answer? The buzzing changed to quick, short bursts. I wanted to open the window and scream at him. Then, suddenly, it stopped.

I stood in the silence, waiting, and when it was shattered by the shrill ring of the phone, I jumped. Dad? The dreaded guidance counselor? When the buzzer started up again, I ran down the hall, shut my door, and pulled a pillow over my head.

CHAPTER EIGHT

Mom's cool hand on my forehead woke me from a dead sleep, my head thick, eyes heavy.

"Have you been crashed out here all day, Addy? You're not hot. No fever ... so, what is it now?" Her voice was tight and clipped.

"Just tired," I murmured, but she'd left the room, heels clicking on the hardwood floor.

I slid off the bed and followed to find her standing in the kitchen staring at the dirty dishes in the sink. The breakfast stuff was still spread over the table. Mom lowered a bag of groceries with a thud.

"Sorry," I muttered. "I guess I forgot to clean up."

She threw her heavy sweater over a kitchen chair and began scraping crumbs off the table with one hand and catching them with the other.

"You didn't go to the school." It was a flat statement, not a question.

I shoved my hands deep in my jean pockets. "I couldn't ... I couldn't seem to ..."

Mom closed her eyes slowly and sucked in a long breath. "Did Mr. Drisdale, the guidance counselor, call?"

"I – not that I know of. I wasn't able to ..."

She tossed the crumbs in the garbage. "Don't bother thinking up an excuse, Addy. You simply ignored the phone, right? I know, because I called you twice – after I got back from a location shot and a bit of shopping to find half a dozen phone messages from Mr. Drisdale on my desk. He said he rang here again and again when you didn't show up. I came home right away, worried sick. Where have you been?"

"I wasn't actually here for most of the morning."

Mom gave me a sharp look. "Oh? Where were you?"

"I went down to ... I had cookies and tea at Harmon's."

"At Harmon's?"

"With the girl who lives upstairs. We all bumped into one another in the hall ... and ... he asked us in for tea, and then I came home and slept. I can't hear the phone in my room –"

"Right." Mom yanked a chair out from the table. "Sit."

"Mom ..." I pleaded.

"What is it, Addy? I know you can manage classes. And you felt well enough to go downstairs for tea and cookies, for God's sake. Yet you were too sick to keep your appointment with the school counselor?"

This was it. I was going to have to tell her.

Stand on your own two feet. Be yourself.

"Mom. I'm not going to school." I was as surprised at my words as she was.

Oh jeez ... what have I done?

She began to unpack the groceries. She put a white deli carton on the table, followed by a loaf of bread. "I know *that,* Addy. That's what we have to talk about: w*hen* you'll go back —"

"No, Mom. I'm not going back to school — ever again." I felt reckless and strangely brave.

She stared at me, blinking rapidly. "What's that supposed to mean? You have to go to school *sometime,* Addy. We just have to work out when, that's all. If you don't finish high school, then what about university?"

I stood my ground. "I don't care about university — that's almost three years away. I'm not going back to that school or any other. And you can't …"

Mom's face went cold and hard. "I can't what?"

"And you can't make me, Mom. I have to do what's right for me."

There. I'd said it. I felt drained of blood. I waited for the ceiling to crash in on me.

Instead, Mom carefully unpacked the rest of the items. Italian salami. Chicken breasts. Cold meats. One by one, they were gently lowered onto the red arborite tabletop. Except for the rustle of plastic, there was absolute silence.

Finally, she shook her head and said, "What's right for you, huh?"

"Yes," I said, defiantly, my knees trembling.

She sighed. "Addy … I've had a shitty afternoon. I'm not up to silly games. If you were actually still sick I might be willing to listen, but —"

"I *am* still sick."

"No, Addy, you're *not*. You're sewing by the hour. Reading books by the dozens. Watching those damn old movies of yours. You don't actually *do anything* – particularly around here to help me – but you *are* better. You're only fifteen. You're going to school and that is final."

I stuck out my chin. "I can make up my own mind. I know if I'm sick or not."

"Then we'll go for more tests and find out for sure."

"No."

Anger ... or was it fear? ... blazed in Mom's eyes. "Then come with me to see the school psychologist," she said slowly and evenly. "The counselor says she's great and –"

I couldn't believe it. "You talked to some stranger about me seeing a shrink? About me being *crazy?*"

"Don't be silly, Addy."

"Stop saying that! As if everything I say is stupid and useless!"

"I'm sorry, honey. It just hurts me that you'd even *consider* thinking I'd tell anyone you're crazy. You're nothing of the sort!"

"Then what am I, in your opinion, Mother?"

"Sharon says ... no, *I think* ... with the move and leaving your friend Jodie, and this tension between you and your dad ... you might want to talk to someone."

"Sharon says? Anybody you haven't talked to? Maybe your buddy Harmon? No, I'm sure you've already told *him* everything! How about the neighbors on either side?"

"Addy," Mom kept her voice low, "... be fair. I'm not the only one who's worried. Your dad's also —"

"Oh yeah, sure he is! Give me a break. And what does *Auntie* Sharon say? Huh? That I'm lazy? That I'm acting out? Not having any kids makes her a frigging expert, right?"

"Addy! Please! I can't do this right now — I've had a terrible day and —"

"If you'd *actually* listen, Mom, you'd hear that I'm talking about *me* right now, okay?" The little jammering thumps were back, the pressure inside my head building. "I'm not going back, Mom. I can make up my own mind. I can do schoolwork at home."

Mom rubbed shaky fingers over her forehead. "Look, Addy. Mr. Drisdale says that you *have* to go to science and French labs to get full credits. And he also says you'll have to write fall exams soon — and you have to write them *at the school.*"

"I'm not stepping foot inside that place again, Mom!"

"Well, then *another* school, Addy. You have to go and that's final."

"Not that school. Not any school. *No school.*" The hammer in my head picked up speed and a white light gathered in front of my eyes.

Stand on your own two feet. Stand on your own two feet!

"Addy. Please, don't do this, okay? I *know* it's been hard. I *know* there have been big changes. But you can't get your own way just by shouting. I'm trying to do my best."

"The day we were leaving, Dad said I was an ungrateful,

spoiled kid. You two agree on *something* at least. Hey! Maybe that'll keep your pathetic excuse for a marriage afloat? Whaddya think?"

Mom shoved the chair against the table with a loud crack. "Don't push it, Addy. Don't bloody push it."

"But you never listen! Just like him!" I cried. "Why don't you listen to me?"

"I am *not* like your father. Don't you ever say that to me. I'm here. He's not!" Her fine auburn hair had slid out of its clip and her face was pale as ash.

I knew I was hurting her, but deep inside a voice of utter certainty made me say once again, "I'm not going back to school. Do what you want, say what you want – *I am not going back.*"

Like a distorted vision in a fun-house mirror, her face went through a variety of expressions. Then, mouth trembling, she glared – as if somehow staring me down would change my mind.

"Mom ... I can't ... please ..." Tears burned my eyes. "I'll make sure I do all the dishes, I'll do all the housework, I'll start making supper. I'll –"

"Oh, Addy! I've been through too much of this. I'm exhausted from worrying. At least *try* to understand that I'm –"

The kitchen shattered before my eyes. With clenched fists I began to slowly, heavily pound my hips. "I'm sorry I'm lousing it all up. I know I've let you down. I know I've been lazy. I *know* I'm a terrible daughter – I know I'm not

making it easier. I know, I know, I know! I'm sorry. *Sorry!*
But I can't ... I can't ... I *can't* ..."

With each of the final words, I pounded my body
harder and harder. A voice inside was telling me to stop,
but I couldn't. I couldn't see, couldn't think. My head was
going to burst.

"Addy! Stop it! You're frightening me! Addy!" Mom
grabbed my arms, but I wrenched free and ran down the
hall, a high shrill sound following me. Who was making
all that noise?

CHAPTER NINE

I felt Mom's hand on my shoulder, but I couldn't stop crying. Eventually, I fell into a thick headachy sleep. When I woke up, the small lamp beside my bed cast a dim glow across the darkness. I turned over to find Mom sitting in shadow on the small rattan chair beside the dresser.

"Hi," she whispered.

I thought I had no more tears left, but I was wrong. "Mom. I'm sorry."

"Don't be sorry, sweetie. You were right. I wasn't listening." She clasped her hands tightly and leaned forward. "What is it, Addy, what's really wrong?"

"I don't know. I just know that I – I can't go back to that school. I can't. I won't."

"But why not, Addy?"

I wanted to tell her how, whenever I tried to leave the house, I felt as if I was going to go crazy or die, but I just couldn't do it. She'd never understand.

"So much has happened, Mom. I just need time. I don't know how else to explain it."

"Addy, those teachers won't be willing to keep sending stuff home. Mr. Drisdale said —"

"I could start home studies — there's something called Distance Education. Jodie used to do that when she lived up north. I saw it on TV last week. Anyone can take it."

"I don't know Addy —"

"Couldn't I try? Just for one term? Just to see how I do? I'll do lots of stuff around here, too. Honest."

She rubbed her face with her fingertips. "It's not just the work, Addy. You need to be with other kids. Meet new friends. Socialize. You need to be … a teenager. I'm worried, honey, really worried that you don't seem to want to leave the house at all."

I swallowed hard. "I — I just figured if I left the house, you'd think I was ready for school. And I can't go back there, Mom. I *can't* —"

"Addy, look, maybe we should at least talk to a counselor before we make this decision — based on reasonable —"

"NO!" My eyes stretched wide. "I told you. I'm not going back."

"Okay, okay, Addy." Mom's face was a pale moon hovering in the darkness. "Look. Let's leave it for a day or two —"

"Why can't I just start with home study for grade ten? I could catch up easily."

Mom closed her eyes. Finally she sighed and said, "All right. I'll look into this correspondence stuff tomorrow. If it looks at all plausible …"

Her words made me dizzy with relief.

I'd won!

I tried not to smile too broadly. "Thanks, Mom. I won't let you down, I promise." I put out my arms. She hugged me hard, then held me by the shoulders and looked deep into my eyes.

"One term, Addy. Just one term. You're too young to drop out of life. It may mean talking to a different kind of doctor. I want you out doing things and –"

"I won't let you down," I promised, hugging her again. Now that I'd got my way, I could finally leave the house.

Couldn't I?

CHAPTER TEN

Mom and I made dinner together. At first I thought our silence was one of harmony, so I told her about the room across the hall and about Page and the crazy parrot and how the voices I'd heard had been real after all. She looked startled at first and then irritated – and I realized I'd trapped myself. I'd found time for that, but not for school.

I told her instead about the boy who'd arrived in the taxi. I could laugh now about being freaked out by the buzzer ringing, but Mom didn't laugh. She glanced over at me, then back at the lettuce, which she tore into pieces with hard twists of her fingers.

She was having second thoughts. My chattering had only made it worse. Good one, Addy.

"Addy, you *do* know that we still have to talk to Mr. Drisdale about your leaving," she said finally. "And what do I tell your dad? He'll be calling very soon."

I stirred a pot of mushroom soup. The soft grayish lumps floating through the creamed broth made me feel sick. Mom was going to have to face people at work with the news that her daughter was a dropout. And Dad would go berserk. Mom could talk all she wanted about not worrying what others thought, but she really *did* care. And that was going to ruin everything.

"But we don't *have* to actually go to the school." I kept my voice as even as I could. "A phone call from you would be enough. And I'll be the one to talk to Dad."

"Really? When you've hardly said two words to him for months?"

She was right. Could I actually be pleasant to him knowing he'd practically ruined our lives?

I'd hated the thought of moving to Winnipeg but had finally come to realize if Mom and Dad were there I could survive anything. For months I'd ignored the fact that they'd been arguing. They'd always argued – not noisy rows, more like hissing, snide little stabs at each other. But as the time drew nearer to the move, their fights had really picked up in frequency and volume.

Then, about a week and a half before take-off, I had come home to both cars in the driveway and a deadly silence as thick as soot throughout the house. Mom was sitting at the kitchen table, looking stunned. When I asked her what was wrong, she'd just pointed to the den.

Dad was slouched in front of the TV. When I cleared my throat, he looked at me, turned off the sound, and said, "I guess you'd better hear this from me, kiddo. Sit down."

He told me that he hadn't quit his job after all – that he'd known all along he wasn't going to leave Toronto – not yet, anyway.

"But you said–" I began.

"Things will work out eventually, kiddo, once your mother understands that this whole thing is completely out of hand. We'll sort it through." And that was that. He wouldn't talk about it anymore, even though I'd begged.

Mom had just hugged me hard and said, "He doesn't get it yet. He will."

It was like they were talking in code, and obviously my opinion didn't count.

They'd sorted it through all right – with frozen silences broken by vicious barbs back and forth, like acid-filled Ping-Pong balls. Everything was out of whack. I could hardly sleep at night for the sickening worry that pulsed through me.

Would Dad really let us go to Winnipeg without him?

He expected Mom to back out of the move, but she soon made one thing perfectly clear – she was going with or without him.

I kept my fingers crossed that Dad would give in. After all, months earlier, he'd told her that he would make the move if she got the right deal with Sharon – a full partnership in the film production company. And she had.

But now he wouldn't give an inch.

Things clattered to rock bottom when Dad cancelled the furniture vans.

"I'll keep the bigger stuff for now," he had said matter-of-factly when I asked him for the millionth time what was happening. "Your mother is going to look for a furnished place."

"What about the house you guys were going to rent?"

"Back on the market. It's easy when you're in the real estate business." He shrugged and walked away.

I knew he was banking on *her* giving in. But she didn't. I listened all that day and the next to frantic phone calls between Mom and Sharon. When Mom announced she'd found a flat for us in an old house, Dad stared at her as if she'd suddenly turned into Daffy Duck. After that he turned into someone else himself – a grim-faced, silent stranger.

Finally, in desperation, about four days before we were to leave, I took the subway to his realty office downtown. I wish I'd found him madly kissing his secretary or something, so I'd have some logical explanation for why he wouldn't transfer to Winnipeg as he'd promised. But of course they weren't in a sordid clinch like some sleazy movie. Dad was sitting behind his desk dictating a letter to skinny gray-haired Mrs. Perdaski, who was scribbling away in her notepad.

He looked up in surprise. "Hi, kiddo. What brings you here? Thanks, Mrs. P. You can finish that up for me, right?"

"So what's up?" Dad said when the door closed behind her. His tone was jovial – his usual salesman's B.S.

"Don't play dumb, okay, Dad?" I snarled. "I want to know why you aren't coming with us." I plunked down on the chair that Mrs. Perdaski had just vacated. "And I'm not leaving until you tell me."

Dad fiddled with some pencils on his desk, lining them up side by side in a neat row. "Addy, your mother doesn't *have* to go *anywhere*. She can get work here. This is just a load of nonsense."

"You know it's a big opportunity for her, Dad. More documentaries are being funded in Manitoba than in any other province right now ... and this new partnership in Sharon's company was a great step –"

"Mother's little echo, huh, Addy? She's brainwashed you very well, indeed."

"Don't you get it, Dad? Mom and I are *going!* You promised you'd come with us! You're copping out!"

"I can't do it, kiddo. I'm sorry."

My throat tightened. "We'll never see you again."

"Don't be silly, Addy! Of course I'll see you. Both of you will be back, I guarantee it."

"How do you know that?"

"Because I know your mother. She's being stubborn, that's all. But after she's been in a frozen prairie town for a few months, she'll see sense. I refuse to risk every-thing I've built here just for one of her whims."

"It's not a whim, Dad."

He sighed. "Addy, when you were ten, Jill worked in radio – for two minutes. Then she decided to go back to school to get her teaching certificate. She taught high school for one semester before quitting. Now she's *into* film."

"So?" I pushed my bottom lip out and narrowed my eyes.

"But for how long, Addy? She actually had me convinced for a while to give up my job here. Her enthusiasms can be quite infectious. But sanity came to me one day as I was driving home. I realized there was a good chance we'd both end up jobless. I can't risk that. Not after all the work I've put in here."

"But, Dad, she'll have a good job in Winnipeg and so could you!"

"I've got a good job here – one I'm successful at." He stood up and adjusted his belt over his sagging tummy. "The real estate industry in the prairies is a joke right now. I don't want my – our – future to be uncertain."

"Uncertain? Whaddya call this, for pete's sake?" I cried. "All you ever do is gripe about work, anyway."

"Addy, that's not true –"

"It *is* true. It is! You always moan about how much you hate it. *Why can't you come with us?*"

"Try to understand …" he started, then shook his head. "Look, let's get one thing straight. You don't have to go anywhere." He leaned forward. "Your mom can try it out, and if she makes a go of it, well … you could move out there later on. Maybe by then, I might –"

"I can't let Mom go on her own. Even if you can!"

"But you're leaving me on *my* own," he said.

"No, I'm not! *You're* choosing to be alone. That's different. You *could* come and be with us. Please, Dad." A terrible pressure inside my head scared me, but I managed to say, "We've always been a family … you can't –"

"We still *are* a family, kiddo. Maybe … maybe I'll come later."

He was lying. I could see it in his eyes.

"Why, Dad?" I cried. "Why are you ruining every-thing!"

He looked stricken. "Look, Addy, I *have* explained. Maybe if you talked to your mom, we could –"

I put my hands over my ears and ran, past a shocked Mrs. Perdaski, past the subway stop, and across a car park into a coffee shop. I sat in a corner booth and ordered a Coke. Only when the waitress brought it and left – only then did I let the hot tears run down my cheeks. Leaving Jodie was bad enough, but knowing Dad's job meant more to him than Mom and me made my insides all tangled up and sore.

I straggled home, just in time to see his car back out of the driveway. I hid behind a tree. He drove past, his face grim, his shoulders stiff. I watched the car grow smaller and disappear.

He just didn't love us enough.

Three days later, at the airport, Mom stood as far away from him as she could. Their eyes never met. I couldn't stand being near either of them. Dad tried to talk to me, and when I wouldn't answer he lost his temper. He called me a spoiled brat and then looked shocked at his own words. I wanted to hurt him then – make him feel the same hollow emptiness, the same ache in his chest that I had in mine, so I'd stalked through the security check without looking back.

And I hadn't seen him since.

CHAPTER ELEVEN

I didn't realize I was standing like a statue until Mom wrapped her arms around me and brought me back to the tiny kitchen on Macmillan Street.

"I won't let you down, Mom," I whispered. "Please don't change your mind."

"I've already agreed, Addy. We'll try it. But like I said — *one* term only." She poured our soup and I sat down across from her.

"Then why do you still look so ... so *miserable?*"

"I don't know. It's as if somehow, now that I've given in, it's okay for you to be cheery and smiley and ..." She shook her head. "I sound like I want *you* to be miserable. And I don't ... it's just ... oh, I don't know."

She stirred her soup, then crumbled a couple of soda biscuits over it.

I was trying hard not to beg. "But this way I can take rests when I want and work when I want, and I'll do all the housework and I'll make dinner and —"

"Okay, okay, I've given in, remember?" She tried to smile. "We'll get to work on organizing these home studies, but take this as a certainty, Addy – we will get you back on track … find someone to talk to, an advisor – agreed?"

"But after a while, okay?"

Mom shook her soup spoon at me. "As long as you get some fresh air and exercise – *outside*."

"I will." I'd lied to Mom more times that day then I ever had in my life. But it was worth it. I'd work hard in the apartment, keep it clean, learn to cook – I'd make up for the lies. Today was Friday. What if she pushed me to go out with her on the weekend? Should I get another 'sore throat' just in case?

Then I remembered.

"Are you supposed to be going out tonight? Harmon said something about meeting you at eight o'clock."

Mom cleared her throat. "I was going to tell you about it. Now I don't know what to do. Money's really tight, Addy. I mentioned to Harmon that I waitressed my way through university, and he suggested I drop by his club tonight – maybe try it for one evening. And if I like it …" She shrugged. "I thought you'd have schoolwork. I can cancel it."

I said quickly, "No. Go ahead. Don't cancel it. I'll be okay."

"It's only from eight to eleven, but the pay's good. Harmon's agreed to waive this month's rent until the funding for this damn film kicks in. I don't want to ask your dad – not at this early stage." She looked at me uneasily. "You're sure you'll be okay?"

A funny mixture of worry and relief swept through me. I hated the thought of being alone all evening, but if Mom was gone she wouldn't be tempted to go on and on about the Decision … or Dad … or that suddenly we didn't have any money.

"I'll be fine. Really," I said. To prove it, I forced down most of my soup and salad and even had a small bowl of chocolate ice cream, and then insisted on doing all the dishes. Mom, after a couple of sidelong glances at me, went to have a shower.

When I was finished, I curled up on the sofa and closed my eyes. They ached deep inside from all the crying. I turned off the lamp and the pain eased a bit. I must have dozed, because before I knew it, Mom was there, zipping up her jacket.

"I'm on my way. I just went to check the mail and saw Harmon in the hall. That boy you were talking about is his son. Harmon's ex-wife has remarried and I guess the boy and her new husband don't see eye to eye. He'll be going to your high school –"

"It's not my school," I said firmly, blinking as she flicked on the overhead light. "And I couldn't care less about Harmon's kid. If you'd heard him ringing that doorbell –"

"Okay, okay," Mom said, "I was only talking."

"Sorry."

"I can stay home if you're not feeling well, honey. It's been tough –"

"I feel okay. Really. Go." I smiled. "You look great, Mom."

"Well, thanks," she said, looking pleased.

Her hair was pinned up with a row of brown tortoise-shell combs, and she wore long silver earrings, pants and a black silky shirt under her tweed suit jacket. But her cheeks were very pale under the light dusting of blush. I felt a strong mix of love and guilt.

"Don't sit in the dark after I've gone, Addy. It's too depressing." Then she sighed. "I had hoped you'd make friends here – to study or go to movies with. But –"

A prickly irritation crept over me. "I don't need friends right now, Mom, believe me. See you later."

She sighed again. "Okay. No tea with caffeine in it, Addy. Harmon gave me some herbal stuff. I put it on the counter. He says it's for you – good for the nerves." She squinted at me as if trying to put pieces of a puzzle together in her head.

"I don't need *nerve tea*," I snapped. "He's such a Nosy Parker. Hey, aren't you going to be late? It's almost a quarter to eight."

She grabbed her big leather pouch and made for the door at a trot. "We'll talk later, sweetie. Night night."

And she was gone with a snap of the lock.

CHAPTER TWELVE

A few seconds later someone rapped softly on the door. Page stood on the other side of the fish-eye peephole wiggling her fingers in the air, and somehow I felt forced to open up. She was carrying a guitar case.

"Hi. I just saw your mom leave and thought I'd come down and ask you – hey – you okay? Your eyes are all red and puffy."

"Just tired."

"I'm fed up with studying," she said. "So, did you meet Sean today?"

"Sean?"

"Yeah, Harmon's kid. I met him in Alberta. He used to come to all our gigs. Wants to be a musician, too. When he heard we were coming to Winnipeg, he told us about his dad renting out cheap flats."

Great. One big happy household. Except me.

"Shouldn't you be at the club?" I asked.

"Not yet. I had to write an essay tonight. I just finished. Josh is picking me up soon. Look, Addy, I need a favor." She jiggled the guitar case. "Can I come in?"

"I guess." I left the door partially open as a hint that she couldn't stay long.

"Oh goodie!" she said, "I've been dying to see what you've done in here. We were going to rent it, but we couldn't afford to. We just have one big room upstairs with a kitchen alcove." She put her guitar on the floor and veered left into the living room. "This is a pretty big house, eh? Imagine one old lady rattling around in it."

Why didn't she just tell me what she wanted and leave? I didn't want to think about that strange Lotta person.

"You sure you're okay?" she said. "You should get a tonic from Harmon. You hardly have any energy for someone so young."

"Right, and you're ancient," I said sharply.

She laughed, that same silly giggle that Victor had imitated so perfectly. "You should ask Harmon if you can borrow some of Lotta's furniture he's got stored. It's pretty bare in here, huh?"

"Mom wouldn't want some old lady's junk."

"It seems a shame to waste her things, that's all. Harmon offered me the loan of some of it, but there's not much space up there. Besides, Josh might forget it doesn't belong to him and … never mind." She looked around the room, one finger pressed against her lips, an assessing look in her eye. "You know, your mom has good taste. Those two chairs – very retro-fifties. Second-hand, right?"

"Yeah … so?"

She picked up one of Mom's Caithness glass paperweights, part of a collection she'd had for years. "Having a good eye helps when you're on a tight budget."

That made me see red. "Harmon's been blabbing about our money problems to you? He has no right!" I snatched the paperweight out of her hand and put it back on the shelf.

"Harmon didn't really say much – honest. When I really like someone – like you for instance – I want to know all about them. I get told off a lot for being nosy. It's a problem for some people. Sorry, Addy."

My anger fizzled. How could you stay mad at someone who's just said she likes you? Especially when you're being a pig. Why couldn't I be that breezy and nonchalant?

"Sorry ... I – you want a Coke or something?"

"No thanks. Josh'll be here any minute."

I stood awkwardly, wondering what to say next. Finally I blurted out, "What kind of music do you play?"

"We're sort of rock-folk. Hey! You wanna come down tonight?"

"No! Uh ... no thanks, I'm really ..."

"No problem. Maybe tomorrow?"

I mumbled, "Yeah, maybe."

She nodded. "Anyway, listen, Addy, I wonder if you'd keep that for me." She pointed at the guitar case at her feet. It was made of heavily tooled black leather and had a number of stickers scattered across it.

"Why?"

"It's my grandfather's. He played in a blues band a zillion years ago. He taught me to play and left it to me when he died last year." Her eyes were sad. "It's the only thing I took when I left home."

"So, why do you want me to keep it?"

She shifted back and forth on her feet. "Well, see —"

The door swung open and banged against the wall. I spun around, stifling a yelp.

It was the boy from the taxi.

CHAPTER THIRTEEN

"Sean!" Page exclaimed. "What are you doing here?"

"I was heading up to your place to say hi. Heard voices. Knew it was you ... so ..." He shrugged. "Why, she got the plague or somethin'?" He looked at me and frowned. "Maybe you do, huh? You don't look so good."

My tongue was stuck to the roof of my mouth. I hated him instantly, with his sharp curious eyes and clipped voice.

"Ignore him, Addy," Page said, but she was smiling at Sean. "So how long are you here for?"

He shrugged. "Who knows?"

"Weren't you living in Edmonton?"

"My mother married a guy straight out of The X-Files, so I decided to split. She was happy enough to see me go, and step-papa practically sang all the way to the airport." He shivered dramatically.

"Is your dad okay with it?"

"Pop? Sure. He's cool. So this apartment finally got rented, huh? Man, this room needs work. Trust Pop to put you in without painting the joint."

"My mother and I still have to choose the colors we want," I said stiffly.

"Yeah? Well, when you do, let your mom know I used to work for College Painters in the summer. I'd do it cheap and I'm the best there is."

Page said, "Somehow I don't think they'll have to pay for it, Sean."

He laughed. "I doubt it'll get done otherwise. My dad's got too many other jobs to do around this pit – and now he's got me in the way, slowing him down. Still, two women in distress might get him going, huh? Pop always was very *gallant*."

I'd never actually met anyone who had *eyes* that laughed.

"You always stand with your mouth open?" he asked. "You won't get your knight in shining armor that way."

I pursed my lips together hard and glared at him.

"Oooh. Scary. If you've got a tongue to match that look, I could disintegrate right where I stand."

"Be my guest," I said, my voice flat.

He patted himself all over. "Have to do better than that. I'm still here."

"Too bad. I'll have to practice."

He sat down on the couch, leaned back, and clasped his hands behind his head. "Better. Keep at it. So … what're you girls up to?"

Page kicked his foot off the coffee table. "Addy and I are talking. I've got to go to your dad's club soon. So go away."

"Can I get a lift over there with you?"

"If you go away … now." She opened her eyes wide and stared at him.

He slowly rose to his feet. "With both of you giving out

the death rays, I definitely can feel my left arm dissolving. No point in asking for a Coke with ice, right? No. I'll just mosey along before I turn to ashes where I stand."

Page rolled her eyes. "Just go, Sean. I don't want to be late."

He ruffled her hair and kept going. Just as he reached the door, he contemplated the guitar for a second or two and then said to me, "Don't forget to tell your mom about painting this place. I could do with the bread."

I sneered. "I don't think so."

He nodded and grinned. "Haven't won you over yet, huh? Well, I'll practice, too. Hey, I bet you go to Kelvin High, right?"

"No," I said. He could go to a new school, no problem. Why couldn't I? I hated him even more.

He shrugged. "Just as well. Every time I passed you in the halls I'd have to duck the killing radar in those spooky black eyes."

When the door closed behind him, I stood there, cheeks hot, heart thumping – but this time it wasn't fear. It was pure hatred.

CHAPTER FOURTEEN

"Sorry, Addy," Page said. "He's actually a nice guy most of the time. You'll really like him when you get to know him."

She picked up the guitar and headed toward the kitchen. "Your bedroom down here?" she called over her shoulder. "Thanks for holding on to this for me. Listen, I'd rather you kept this to yourself, okay?"

By the time I gathered my wits enough to follow her, she was rummaging in my closet.

"Hey!"

"Oh ... sorry. Look, just put it anywhere no one will see it, okay?" She touched my arm. "It's the only thing I have that I can't lose, Addy. It keeps me close to Gramps, you know?"

"Why do you want to leave it here?" I asked. "Why not somewhere where no one goes – like Victor's room?"

Page shrugged. "I'd rather it was where someone will keep an eye on it. I'll make sure Sean keeps his trap shut about seeing it."

"Why?"

She looked as if she'd said too much. She flapped her hand at me and said, "You don't need to know."

"Why not? Why can't you tell me?"

"It's just something you don't need to know about, okay?"

Flushed with anger, I said, "Fine, don't tell me. I never know what anyone means anymore, anyway. There's all these secrets *out there* and no one wants to let me in on them. Everyone does it. Kids at school. My parents. That jerk Sean. So why not you? Keep your little secret, but don't expect me to keep that thing here, okay?"

Page put the guitar on the bed and sat down beside it. "Hey, Addy, I'm really sorry. It's just that ..." She took a deep breath. "Okay. Josh and I took it to a music store to have some work done on it, and the repair guy went nuts. I knew Gramps was well known, but I had no idea that he was actually *famous* in jazz circles. Even the case is a collector's item ... and ... well, Josh wants me to sell them both. But I just can't, you know?"

"Why don't you simply tell him he can't sell it? It's yours."

She shrugged. "He's ... very impulsive. If he needs money, he'll do anything to get it ... but he usually regrets it later. Please, Addy. I trust you."

"You don't even know me."

"There are some people that you just *know* you can trust."

I gave up. She was going to get her way, even if she had to B.S. me. "Okay, okay ... just leave it here. But if it gets lost or stolen I'm not paying for it."

She smiled. "Thanks, Addy."

We sat for a second or two, Page taking in my messy room with her curious eyes, me trying to think of something to say.

"Did you do that embroidery thingy on the wall?" she asked, peering at it.

"It's needlepoint. And yeah ... but it's not very good." After seeing Lotta Engel's work, I was ashamed that I'd had the nerve to frame such an ugly thing. It was a stilted, overly bright picture of an English cottage with stiff flowers and a thatched roof that looked like a block of maple fudge which always hung crooked, as if the roof was so heavy it pulled one side down. She reached up to straighten it with both hands and I saw them – the marks I was sure I'd seen earlier that day. On her right arm was a tattoo of a bluish hand with pale pink nails. The fingers were wrapped around Page's slender forearm, about four inches above the wrist. As if sensing she was being watched, she dropped her arms so the sleeves covered the peculiar markings, but not fast enough to hide the fact that the other arm had real bruises – dark purple fading to tinges of green scattered up and down her pale skin.

"Did it hurt to have that done?" I blurted out. "What does the hand mean?"

"What?" Page asked, as if she hadn't heard.

"That tattoo."

"Oh, that. I had it done after I met Josh. We each have one – his hand on my arm and mine on his."

"You've known each other a long time?"

"Not that long – but we connected right away. I was busking out in Victoria and he liked my voice and my songs. And I liked the look of him, so ... we teamed up."

"What's busking?"

She smiled indulgently and began to touch things on my dresser – the antique silver brush and mirror set Mom gave me, my collection of old perfume bottles. "You have lived a sheltered life, haven't you? Busking is street peddling – but with an act. Magic, mime, dancing, singing, juggling. I was working with another girl, Pat. She played guitar, too. I wrote the songs. Gramps and I used to make up all sorts of ditties – that's what he called them. My dad said I had no talent, but I do – that's one thing I've always been sure of. Gramps told me."

"You actually lived on the street?"

"Sure. Vancouver Island has *great* weather. There's some decent soup kitchens in Victoria, and we slept in welfare flats – sometimes fifteen kids in one room."

"But you had a home and parents and all, right?"

"Yeah. In Regina. And a brother who's a med student and a sister who's probably a lawyer by now. I'm the Family Failure. No good to anyone. So why not give them what they wanted? I split."

"They wouldn't want you to live on the streets, would they?" I couldn't even walk two blocks to school. How could she leave home having nowhere to go? It was mind-boggling.

"All I knew for sure was they didn't want me around."

"I always thought that only abused kids ran away. Like if their dads beat them up or — you know — other stuff."

Page looked at me with pity. "There are other ways of beating someone up besides using your fists, Addy. Lots of ways. There's the kind that eats at your guts — at who you are as a person, like your soul, you know? Me and my dad were always screaming at each other. Everything I did was stupid or ridiculous or wrong. So why should I live in a place where I can't be ... who I am?"

"How could the street be better than home?"

"It's being free of all that hassle, you know? I didn't wake up every day knowing I was going to disappoint someone. I met good friends on the street. We watched out for each other. I'd probably still be there except I started getting sick a lot and pretty much stayed in an area where there was a free clinic. It was near a club where Josh was playing."

"That's how you met him?"

"Yeah. His band wasn't doing all that well. He wanted me to sing with them. My own songs." She laughed. "I don't know what he saw in me then. I was wearing a scarf around my head all the time because I'd been losing my hair and I had skin problems. But my voice has always stayed clear and strong."

"You were losing your hair?" I asked, not quick enough to cover my shock.

"Yeah. I kinda got into drugs. You kid yourself that it's natural to use them. I mean, I wasn't particularly unhappy

— I wasn't *anything*. But then Josh talked me into making a change. Sounded like a bit of a blast. So why not? The guys thought Josh was nuts. But — surprise! — we've been together for almost five months. I'm clean, too, thanks to him. And we've started getting some good-paying gigs. Our last place was Edmonton. Josh decided to come to Winnipeg because there's some great clubs here. We found this apartment through Sean. I liked his dad right away. In fact, Harmon's the one who convinced me to go back to school."

"He did?"

"Yeah. He suggested — and when Harmon suggests something it's like an order from an army general — anyway, he *suggested* I try a summer course in music. Told me I had to get some independence on file. I did really well, too, even though I barely scraped through high school. Now I'm taking a few more classes. I try to save every penny."

"Josh must be proud of you, eh?"

"Weeell … he doesn't like the school thing all that much. He's worried it will interfere with the band, but I won't let it. He …" she hesitated.

"He what?"

"He's been kinda holding back part of my take each night, so I'm not saving as much as I'd like to. But this year's courses are paid for at least."

"Josh is stealing from you?"

"No way! I think he just worries that I'll spend it all on school and end up quitting the band. I won't quit, but …

I'd just like to finish this year, you know? Before we move on. That's all." Then, in a quiet voice, she added, "I promised Gramps I'd graduate from music school one day. I'll probably never finish. I usually let people down eventually."

She let people down? Could she really believe that?

"So what about you?" she asked. "When are you going back to school?"

What could I say? That *my* bid for independence was hiding in the house taking home-study courses? That I was a pathetic mess, afraid to go to a real school? That I was totally, utterly hopeless? It took me a second or two to realize she'd continued talking. "Wha– what did you say?"

"I said, I didn't notice how late it was. I gotta go …" She walked out of the room and down the hall. "So you're gonna come to the club tomorrow night, right?" she called over her shoulder.

"I don't think so. I'm not going to the high school anymore – it's too … anyway, I probably won't be able to get out much. Mom brought me my home-study stuff today, so … I've got a lot of catching up to do." I was lying but I didn't care.

At the door, she turned and faced me. In the dim light, her short blond hair stood around her head like fine silver tinsel. "But it's the weekend. Maybe you and I could go to an early movie, and then you could have a pizza while you listen to the band. You won't be studying all weekend will you?"

"I'm still not feeling well enough to –"

"But you said you'd come. It would be fun —"

"I just *can't,* okay?"

A shadow flickered across her eyes, but before she could say anything else, someone hammered on the door.

Page opened it. "Josh! How did you know I was up here?"

A tall, very dark, very handsome, very angry guy with a smooth black beard and shoulder-length hair stood on the threshold. He looked past her, his eyes moving up and down my body. His half smile when he took in my flaming cheeks made me glad I didn't have to speak. When he looked at Page his expression darkened again.

"Harmon's kid said you were up here. I told you that you could stay home and finish your paper as long as you were on the doorstep at nine-oh-five." He held his watch up to her face. "It's nine-oh-nine. Not nine-oh-five. We've got a half hour before the first set. Move it. Let's go, let's go!"

Page turned into a little girl being scolded. "I'm sorry, Joshy. I'll be two seconds."

"Not even one second, Page. Now!" His dark eyes glittered.

He glanced at me and smiled, and something melted inside me. "You comin', too, gorgeous?"

I shook my head, tongue-tied.

He laughed and thumped down the stairs. He'd just made fun of me. My toes curled inside my sneakers.

Page attempted a tight little laugh. "Everything has to be exactly on time with Josh. Good thing. I'm no good with times ... anyway, see you tomorrow?"

"Page! Now!" a voice boomed.

Suddenly her thin arms wound around me, as if she didn't want to let go. Then with a quick brush of lips across my cheek, she was gone.

I watched their old van clatter down the street, then turned on the TV, but my thoughts couldn't focus on the in-your-face noise of the sitcom characters. I played the day over and over again in my head, from Dad's phone call to my fight with Mom, to Page's strange good-bye.

One thing was clear, I hated both Josh and Sean – Josh for being so handsome, so sure of himself. He'd called me gorgeous, and for one moment I'd actually fallen for it. What an idiot I was.

And that Sean – he was the typical sarcastic jerk you find at any school, the kind who thinks he's a stand-up comic. Now I had one more reason to avoid Attila the Bald – the Bad Seed was living with him.

But I couldn't figure out Page. One minute she was full of laughter and confidence, then as soon as Josh arrived, she'd turned into a clingy little kid. What was tonight all about anyway? Did she really want to be my friend? Not likely. She'd just used me to store her precious guitar. Now she wouldn't bother with me. And why should I be surprised?

"Who'd actually *want* to be friends with Addy Jarrick – Miss Nobody of the World?" I asked out loud. When I reached down and banged my hand against the TV's off switch, something moved near the window. A sizzle of fear shot down my legs. I stopped breathing.

A flurry of huge snowflakes floated past the big window. I let out a hiccup of laughter. I *was* losing it. They reminded me of a Christmas ball we used to put out every year. It was a glass bubble filled with water, and when you shook it, white flakes swirled around a little gold and white angel locked inside its tiny space. Like that angel behind bars in Lotta's tapestry. Like me. Except it felt as if someone kept flip-flopping my little world so the turmoil and whirling bits couldn't settle.

The light from the street lamp silhouetted the oak tree. Its leaves were pasted with thin layers of white. I cranked the window open a crack, and a soft howling wind skittered past. Snow scattered off the sodden leaves in soft clumps.

I pulled the window shut and stood in a muffled silence broken only by faint gurgles from the hot water radiator.

Suddenly, there was a distant rumble outside, and a car, packed with kids, roared down the street. It careened around the corner, tires screeching; and as its roar grew faint, an even darker loneliness filled the room. I'd never be with a group of kids like that, going out for a night of dancing and fun. I would always be alone.

Always, always alone.

CHAPTER FIFTEEN

As I walked toward my room, I heard a faint voice call out from behind our front door. The hairs on my arms prickled. I was alone in the house. Wasn't I? Suddenly a loud shriek was followed by a bloodcurdling cry.

"Victor," I muttered through my teeth. The shrieks grew in intensity. Was he in trouble? Leaving the chain on the door, I opened it a crack.

"I need you, girl! Girl! Come here! Girl!"

So he wasn't being attacked by a rabid squirrel – he was just being bossy. As I closed the door, he cried, "I neeeed youuuu!"

"Well, I don't need you!" I snapped the lock and quickly walked to my bedroom, kicked off my sneakers, and started to undress.

What if he was in trouble – maybe his foot was caught or something – or maybe he needed water? He'd just have to wait until morning. I took the small gold hoops from my ears and dropped them on the dresser. The key to Victor's room lay next to my own, attached to the red elastic wristband. I stared at the keys for a long time, then snatched them up, walked back to the door, and listened. If he called again, I'd go – if he kept quiet, I'd go to bed.

"Girl? That you? They come get me. Help me," came a rasping demand.

"Probably the little birds in the white coats come to drag you away to the nut birdhouse," I called back.

I left both doors wide open in case I needed to make a quick retreat. Lotta's room was dark except for Victor's dim light.

"'Bout time," he muttered, glaring at me through the white rings around his sharp little eyes. "Time is of the essence. Essence is the time. Gotta make time. Time goes by, as long as I haaaave youuuuu!" He started to sing in a high falsetto.

I snickered. I was so tired I was punchy.

His feathers went up around his neck, and in that eerie smooth voice, he said, "And what may I ask is so funny?"

"Sorry," I began, then remembered I was apologizing to a bird.

"And well you should be," he intoned.

"You are amazing. How can you talk like this?"

"Victor smart, smart boy."

"And very very spooky. Aren't you supposed to have your cover on?" I asked. "Did Harmon forget? You want me to put it on?"

"Cover up. Life is a cover-up," he screeched. "Cover your eyes. Cover your feelings. Don't cover me up."

I'd let him stew in his own lunacy. I was turning to leave

when I realized I'd forgotten to put the little sheet of cotton over the unfinished angel picture. It would get dusty.

In the light from the hallway, I could see that something was different. The design had been worked on. The area below the feet was filled with twisting ribbons of dark colors, as if the night air had been stirred by a wind. The wings had been worked on, too, with dull, soft grays like Victor's feathers. As I leaned closer, the newly worked areas faded and dissolved, leaving the half-finished angel exactly as it had looked in the afternoon. Victor shifted on his perch and stared at me through the gloomy light, his shabby head tilted as if listening.

A soft creaking sound was followed by a breathy moan. I was about to tell Victor to give it a rest when the door slammed with a crack that sent me across the room. Instinctively, I hid behind a wide bookshelf. Someone was *definitely* in the house – maybe even in this room. But how? The front door had an alarm system that Harmon activated when he went out at night. How come there was no alarm sounding through the house? Had Page forgotten to set it?

I crouched close to the baseboard and waited, blood pounding in my ears. A faint tapping began above me. Victor was chewing on one of the metal bars of his cage. He said in a rattled whisper, "They here. Softly, softly, little mousy."

Who was here? Why was he telling me to be quiet? I peered around the bookshelf. The room was empty. I was about to strangle him with my bare hands when something moved near the center of the room, a dark shadowy shape that floated toward the worktable. I pressed my shoulder against the cold wall. Barely audible at first and then growing in volume, two people began to speak. I was too afraid to look again, so I lowered my bottom onto the floor, scrunched up my knees, and listened hard.

"If you'll just sign the damn house over to me, Lotta, you can still live here," a man's voice said. "That way, if you end up in that ... hospital again —"

A woman answered, her voice weary. "I told you, Freddy, you have no business poking in my affairs. You're my cousin, not my keeper. I'm almost thirty-two years old. I won't be going back to that place again — ever."

"You have no way of knowing that, Lotta. You were out of your mind for months — you had shock treatments. Your brain was fried. You weren't right in the head even as a kid — imagining you saw things before they happened. How can you possibly handle your own affairs?"

"Frederick," the woman said, "you no longer have my power of attorney. My new doctor has given me my life back. It's 1974, not the dark ages! I *can* control my own life! I'm even working again — but not on *them* ... the angels. They chose to betray me. They chose to leave me. But I sew other things. My new work has healed me. I'm *fine*."

"Ridiculous! You've never been fine, never been *normal*. You were always a sick little creature as a child. You found out Engel means 'angel' and you decided this was significant in some way. Look at you! You're a grown-up and you're still talking about them as if they're real. *Now* you say they're *betraying* you? *Leaving* you? It simply shows me how unstable you still are. Lotta, please, for your own sake, let me take over the house. I promise you can live here as long as you want."

The woman's voice was firm. "Go back to Toronto, Freddy. You don't want to *buy* the house, do you? You want me to *give* it to you. How long will it be before I'm out on the street?"

"I would never do that!"

She laughed, a deep bitter sound. "You forget, Freddy, that I, of all people, know you – better than you know yourself. I may have had my brains fried – I may have lost my angels and my second sight – but even shock treatments didn't let me forget what makes you tick! You won't steal the only safe place I know."

"You're paranoid! Crazy!" the man blustered. "I could have you declared incompetent – unable to cope."

"Oh, go away, Freddy. I can more than cope."

"Is that so? Tell me, Lotta, can you leave this house yet? Do you still have your groceries delivered? Still order your clothes over the phone? You see, I know *you!* You've become a bloody *hermit!* You're sick, Lotta. You have no friends. You have little money. I'll buy the house and that would give you an allowance –"

"Go home, Freddy. Just go away and leave me alone."

"To what? To your own madness? So you can go back to all that garbage about guardian angels and visions?"

"'Make friends with the angels, who, though invisible, are always with you,'" she said gently. "Yes, that's what I used to believe. But I don't believe anymore, Freddy. They've turned their backs on me. I can't hear them."

The man was silent for about ten beats, then said, "If I go back to Toronto, I will *also* turn my back on you. If you come begging, you won't find me!"

I waited for her response. I could see Victor sitting very still in his cage, head cocked, beak open. Could he hear them, too?

The woman's voice finally came, distant and thin. "Freddy, what have you become? Don't you ever think of my mother and father? Of Becca? Or Eli? You promised you would tell them. Warn them. You promised!"

"I don't know what you're talking about!"

"Of course you do. I was stuck in the hospital, with appendicitis. You came to visit me."

"Only because your mother begged me. Every time I turned around I was lumbered with you. It wasn't as if you were a kid anymore!" he growled. "You and your nonsense."

"Father said they'd only miss one visiting day – to go for a drive in the country. But, Freddy! I knew what was going to happen! No one in the hospital would listen. You didn't believe me. We could have stopped them. But you didn't even try."

The man's voice was tight. "You couldn't have stopped anything!"

"It's been three years with no one – not even my angels

— to talk to. You should have listened, Freddy. You should have listened!"

Suddenly the door slammed again and again with resounding crashes that billowed like shock waves. Then silence hummed through the room.

I slowly edged forward on my knees until I could see a corner of the worktable and a strip of light across the floor. My scalp tightened. That light meant the door wasn't shut. It hadn't been slammed over and over again. Unless ... it had been my own door?

Was that man in my apartment?

CHAPTER SIXTEEN

I tiptoed forward and peered through the open door. My apartment door was still open. I couldn't hear anything but my own breathing and, now and again, Victor shifting in his cage.

He leaned his head against the bars and said in the smooth woman's voice, "Please don't go, girl. I need you. We need you. It's what you need, too. Don't you see? We need each other."

The voice sounded exactly like the one I'd just heard talking to that awful man.

I couldn't bear it one more second. What should I do? Where should I go? I threw the cover over Victor. He banged around inside the cage muttering vague curses. I stood in the hallway facing my own doorway for a few moments, then ran downstairs and checked the alarm system. The green light was blinking. No one had come into the house. I ran back upstairs and slid through my open door.

Everything was still.

I crept silently down the hall. The back door was locked. I checked closets, looked under the sofa and my bed and even in the kitchen cupboards before locking first the door to Victor's room and then to my apartment. All the time I felt a prickling up and down my neck, expecting someone to speak or a door to crash shut somewhere in the house.

I put on my earphones as soon as I got to my room and turned up the volume. Even Jann Arden couldn't stop me from thinking about Lotta and Freddy. What had Lotta meant about having him warn her parents? Warn them about what?

Did I really want to know?

I tried hard to let the music distract me from my jumbled thoughts, but Arden's lyrical voice was singing about angels, too. "An angel has no armor/Now torn and bent, no wings unfurl/We are looking for it/Oh we are looking for it now …"

Not me. I wasn't looking for angels. Lotta Engel seemed to have found them – the man said she thought she could talk to them – that she knew things before they happened. He meant she was crazy, that's what! That's why she'd been in a mental hospital. Great. I was living in a crazy woman's house and her ghost was hanging around talking.

To me? Was she using Victor to talk to me?

If anyone needed a guardian angel it was Addy 'Nutcase' Jarrick. I ripped off the earphones.

The silence was downright deafening. I undressed quickly. In the dim light beside my bed, I could see a spatter of bruises along my hips. A horrible embarrassed shame swept through me.

It was sick ... really sick.

I crawled into bed and searched under the blankets for Biddy. "Why is everything so mixed up inside me?" I asked her. "Why can't I tell what's real and what isn't?" But she just gazed up at me with her one glass eye and dopey stitched grin. I turned out my light and tried to swallow down sobs which broke through in deep harsh gasps. But the knot of pain stayed in the center of my chest – so deep and so hard that even crying wouldn't dissolve it.

At first I thought I was hearing my own tears echoing, but then I realized that someone else was crying nearby – soft choking sobs in the darkness – echoing my pain. I hardly dared to breathe until the soft scrape of a chair and the rustle of fabric made me sit straight up, eyes bulging.

Then nothing. I turned my light back on. Just me. Alone.

A car door slammed outside. Someone laughed and that set our neighbor's dog barking. I leaned over and looked out the window. The man and woman were greeting their tail-wagging, running-in-circles terrier. That's what I'd heard crying. The dog.

Snowflakes drifted past my window. Fifteen minutes later, the comforting glow of the neighbor's lights turned dark and I lay wide-eyed and locked in empty misery. When I finally heard Mom's key in the lock, I quickly turned onto my side, away from the hall light, and forced my breathing to be slow and regular.

A moment later, Mom crept into my room, fussed with the blanket, and then she did what she always did now...

she sighed, only this time it caught in her throat and turned into a tiny sob, cut off by pressing her fingers over her mouth. Mom did that when she laughed too loud or when she cried, as if she was embarrassed by her own feelings. The click of her boots left the room, and when the hall light went out, another voice drifted from the kitchen.

"Please don't let that be *Auntie* Sharon," I whispered in Biddy's ear.

A burbling laugh echoed along the hall. *Sharon*. She must have met up with Mom after work.

I slid out of bed and peered around the corner. Cold air streamed down the hall and bit my bare ankles. Snorkel Sharon was leaning against the side of the counter, blowing cigarette smoke toward the open back door.

She was wearing a black velvet shirt that hung to her hips and black tights over thick thighs. Her silvery-black hair was tied up in a wild, messy pile, and she wore heavy silver earrings that almost touched her shoulders.

Mom hated smoking, but with Sharon she always compromised. I hated the way Sharon did it – with two or three little puffs each time she put a cigarette to her lips. The cold air reeked of it.

"You worry too damn much, Jill," she said, flapping her hand through a gray billow.

"I can't help it, Shar," said Mom. "She's always been such a good kid – wanting to please, getting good grades. But she just never made friends – until this Jodie kid. And what did I do? I took her away from Jodie and everything familiar and … now she refuses to go to school, plain and simple. Wally'll go ballistic when he finds out."

"You can't put up with this crap, Jill. Your work will suffer." Puff, puff. "Why not just leave Addy alone – she'll soon get bored when she figures out her little games don't work."

My stomach tightened. What games?

I hated her so much.

Mom put two mugs on the table. "She isn't playing games, Sharon. Look, I shouldn't have said anything about it. It's not fair to Addy."

Sharon took a longer drag and finished off with a loud gusty snort. "You *are* being manipulated, Jill. Okay, so Addy got the flu. But then she saw her opportunity and she's stretched it out for weeks. She's trying to *guilt* you into going back home. The doctor couldn't find anything wrong. Are you surprised?"

"Yes, quite frankly, I am. I know her, Sharon. She really *was* sick. There's this virus – Barr Epstein – Julie at work told me about it. You know, Chronic Fatigue Syndrome. It's very difficult to detect, and it can last for months … even years. And it often has emotional side effects."

"Addy doesn't have chronic fatigue, Jill. She's up and about, and she even spent a morning visiting that strange guy from the pub – your landlord – what's his name. Now *that's* something I'd put a stop to right away."

Mom's voice grew higher. "Don't be an idiot, Sharon. Harmon's a nice guy. And he really listens, you know? I'm worried sick about Addy – and now you're saying I should worry about him too? No way!"

"Yeah, I'm sorry. Look, I know Addy's a good kid. Get her this special school work if it will make her happy – give her time to think. It'll work out. I just want you to have your mind on the film."

"I'll concentrate on my work, don't worry," Mom said. "But I can't ignore what's happening to Addy – not for *any* film."

"These are the times I'm glad I never had kids," Sharon said. "Give me a nice cozy editing room any day. Don't be mad at *me* – be mad at my big mouth."

Mom laughed and blew her nose. "Yeah, okay. But you're way off base about Addy."

"I hope so, Jill. I hope so."

I crawled back under the covers. So far, at least, Mom believed me – about school ... and about being sick.

That's when a small voice inside me said *You lied to Mom so that she'd let you stay home and do home studies, didn't you? Now, she'll expect you to go Out There. And what will she say when you don't go? What then? Another lie from you? Sharon is right. You are playing games. You're a devious, scheming liar.*

I might have been able to lie to Mom and get away with it, but I couldn't lie to myself any longer. The truth was I would never be able to stop the fear. I would never be able to go Out There. I'd never be well again.

Never.

CHAPTER SEVENTEEN

A noise, like an engine, was humming in my ears. Was I asleep or awake? It was so dark. As if through a small tear in a black curtain, a man's hands appeared, holding a steering wheel. Oh no! Didn't Freddy tell them? He promised! Warn them! I tried to call out, but the roaring of the engine grew louder and louder. Then there was a long screeching wail, and the crash of metal against metal. The black curtain dropped away, and I stood in a long, poorly lit corridor broken by a row of doors. One of the doors was right behind me. I turned the handle. It was locked. Afraid to bang on it in case it caught someone's attention, I stood rooted to the cold floor, sick with fear.

Where could I go? There was a turn in the corridor ahead. Maybe the exit was that way. Just as I made the turn, I almost bumped into a thin woman with short dark hair. My heart lurched. The woman put one hand up to her mouth in shock and quickly turned away, pressing herself against the wall. She was dressed in a grubby hospital gown. Attached to her back was a pair of bedraggled paper wings roughly cut from newspaper. A length of string held them around her thin rib cage.

Where was I? Who was this woman? I watched my fingers reach out for her shoulder as if they belonged to someone else. When they were almost touching her, she turned her head, and for one brief moment, we looked at each other. Her large black eyes told me everything, that she didn't want to be afraid anymore – that she didn't want to be alone anymore.

"Stay with me," she whispered. "Don't leave me."

Someone appeared and put his hands on her shoulders. Slowly they moved away. The man opened the only door along that corridor and gently pushed her inside. Then he locked it. His keys jangled like chirping birds as he moved into the darkness, his gray wings dragging along the floor.

Behind the small barred window in the door, a pale hand hovered. Lying in its palm were bundles of colored threads, like a small pile of jewels. I reached out and my hand passed right through the bars. As soon as my fingers touched the threads, colors flooded the hallway, flashing around the walls. The floor opened and I fell straight down, dragging the trail of colors with me.

CHAPTER EIGHTEEN

Morning. And I was in my own bed. That long dark corridor, the young woman – it had been a dream.

"You okay, sweetie?" Mom asked from the doorway. She was in her old flannel housecoat, the hair dryer dangling from one hand.

I ran up to her and hugged her hard for defending me against Sharon's accusations. "I'm okay," I lied. "You go get dressed. I'll make breakfast. You want french toast?"

She smoothed back my bangs and kissed me between the eyes. "Sounds great. I'll be exactly ten minutes. I'm going to have to go into work for a little while – but not until later on. Sharon's arranged a meeting, darn her. You'll be okay?"

I hesitated, then said, "Sure. I'll be fine."

As she walked down the hall, she shouted, "Do you believe this snow? Look outside. Unreal!"

I dressed in sweats, heavy socks and fur-lined slippers. My hands were all thumbs, and I had to try twice to wrangle my hair into its single braid. I was still rattled by that strange dream. Was that Lotta? In the mental hospital? I probably only dreamed it because her cousin Freddy said she'd been put in a hospital after –

I stopped. *Demented*. That's what I was. As if I'd actually heard them talking. *Deranged*.

The kitchen was icy cold. I turned on the little heater and beat eggs, added milk, grated nutmeg, and then dipped big chunks of bread into the mixture. I made extra. I'd have the rest for lunch with cream cheese and jam. I sure didn't feel like eating right now. I never could when I was this jittery. While the slices of bread browned, I looked out the window in our back door, which led onto a landing and the narrow flight of wooden stairs. I could see Harmon in the little yard, with a big corn broom, gently dusting the snow off his herbs. He had on black sweats, snowmobile boots and a heavy sweater with a green reindeer design on the back.

Funny how everything looked different this morning – maybe it was the glistening snow, maybe it was relief at having survived those weird dreams, but I'd swear my eyes were sharper. I could see things I hadn't noticed before – like the bright blue birdhouse attached to Harmon's garage and how he'd painted the slats of his fence two different shades of creamy violet. And how the spaces between the slats were bluish white from the snow – giving the whole thing a soft rhythm. For the first time in my life, I felt a need to set down the things I was seeing ... record them somehow.

"Mmm. Smells yummy." Mom had on a red plaid skirt, black tights and a black turtleneck sweater.

"You look really ... young today, Mom."

She laughed and gave me a hug. "Well thank you, Addy, my child."

I put plates on the table along with syrup. The kettle began to whistle. Suddenly I was hungry. I felt good. Something warned me not to examine this feeling too closely though.

"Should we try some of Harmon's tea?" Mom asked. "Can't do much harm, can it?"

"Someone should tell him winter is here," I laughed. "He's outside clearing snow off his plants."

Mom looked flustered for a moment. "Oh? Is he? That's nice."

We had just sat down when we heard someone clumping up the back stairs. Speak of the Bald Devil.

"Hi," Mom said, opening the door.

He grinned broadly. "Brought up the Saturday paper. I know you don't get it, but I've read it and —"

"Come in." Mom's voice was high and light. "You want a cup of your own tea? Or I can make coffee."

Harmon was already inside, shrugging off his thick sweater. "Tea's fine. Smells good. Maple syrup?"

I grimaced. "Fake maple syrup."

"Good enough. I'll have a couple of what you're having." He sat down at the table and looked around. "Man, this room needs doing up badly, huh? I let some old geezer down the street wallpaper and paint in here. A rush job, but I never realized how really bad it was. I'll have to get on it."

Mom passed him a plate loaded with toast and poured his drink. "Addy and I can manage, if you pay for the supplies. I'm good at decorating – I did our whole house in Toronto. Wally said it was —" She looked uncomfortable.

"Hey, Jill, it's my job. I'm the landlord."

Mom put her hands on her hips. "Are you saying you could do a better job? Have you ever wallpapered anything?"

"Well, no, but ..."

As they bickered good-naturedly, I tried to figure out how to ask Harmon about Lotta. I decided to plunge right in.

"Did Lotta Engel live in this house as a kid?"

Harmon stopped in mid-sentence and looked at me.

"Addy," Mom said, "we were talking."

"Sorry."

"That's okay, Addy," Harmon said. "Yeah, I believe she did."

"Did you ever hear about a cousin of Lotta's named Freddy?"

He thought for a moment while he chewed. "No. Can't imagine who'd know that now. She had no living relatives when she died. It was a close neighborhood at one time. But even old Mrs. Grimes is gone now – she knew Lotta's mother quite well. I don't know much at all – except ..."

"Except what?"

"Well, Mrs. Grimes loved a good gossip. She lived around here for years and said that Lotta had quite a reputation for being ... odd ... even as a young girl."

"Odd? How?"

"Apparently she had second sight."

"Second sight? What's that?"

"It's somebody who's psychic. Apparently she appeared to have a kind of supernatural ability to see and hear things others couldn't. According to Mrs. Grimes, so many folks started to come to the house regularly to have Lotta tell them what the future held, that her mother tried to turn them away. But Lotta's father thought it was a gift from the angels and made her talk to everyone."

A gift from the angels?

"That sounds like a cruel thing to do to a young girl," I heard Mom say.

Harmon nodded. "Apparently the father was a bit of a dreamer, too."

"Addy? Are you okay?" Mom asked.

"Huh? Yeah. I'm okay." I began to cut my toast into smaller pieces.

"By the way, Addy," Harmon said, "I saw Page at the club last night and she told me you've got the spare key to Victor's room. May as well hold on to it."

I sat forward. "That room ... I think it was a kind of *studio*."

"Because of all that sewing junk?"

"She did lots of tapestries. That's what's in those brown paper parcels."

"Really? I haven't bothered to check that stuff out. No time." He smiled at me. "Hey, maybe you could make use of it. You do needlework, right?"

"How do *you* know?" I asked, then frowned at Mom.

He smiled. "Yeah, your mom told me. But if you don't use Lotta's things, they'll go to waste."

Mom said, "You told me you'd been in that room next door, Addy, but you didn't say you were actually thinking of using it."

I shook my head. "I'm not."

"Well, I could certainly do with more space. I'll use it."

"NO!" I cried. "It's mine!" My voice sounded loud and shrill in the small room.

Mom sighed and looked at Harmon apologetically. "Make up your mind, Addy. It's very generous of Harmon. And I do need a room of my own."

"You can have my bedroom," I said. "I'll take the one across the hall."

What was I saying?

I almost gasped in relief when Mom said, "Well, we've got lots of time to decide. No matter what, Harmon, we should pay you for it. It's only fair."

"How about a trade? Addy feeds Victor for me and makes a list of everything in there," he said, "and she can use it rent free."

"I – I don't know ..." I murmured.

Mom interrupted. "Wait a minute – who's Victor?"

Harmon chuckled. "A bedraggled old misery-guts of a parrot."

Mom laughed. "Ah yes, the parrot. I didn't realize he had a name, though. I'll have to meet this Victor. I can even feed him, if you like."

I scowled at her. "I'll feed him. I'm the one with the key."

"Perhaps one day you'll introduce us, Addy," she said formally, but she was smiling.

I turned up my own lips, but I didn't put any heart into it. I'd cornered myself. Now I'd have to go next door all the time – maybe I'd even given up my own bedroom. *What was I doing?* What difference did it make if Mom used it? I was acting as if that room was my territory and I had to keep it safe, without even knowing *why*.

I really *was* losing it.

When they started talking again, I didn't pay any attention until I heard Harmon say "– and you know Addy better than anyone. It's probably a good idea for one term."

"You think so?" Mom looked both pleased and uneasy. "My hus– Walter thinks I've made a big mistake."

"What are you guys talking about?" I asked.

Harmon swallowed the last piece of his toast. "You – and home schooling. But, I have no business putting in my two cents."

I leaned forward. "You just said it sounded like a good idea."

He looked at Mom. "Well, Addy, that's just *my* opinion. It's up to your parents."

Mom leaned against the counter, her arms wrapped across her chest. "Harmon's right. It's up to Dad and me."

"And Harmon thinks it's a *good idea*," I insisted. "It's nice to know that not everyone thinks it's weird."

"I don't think it's weird, Addy." She glanced uncomfortably at Harmon.

He shoved back his chair and said, "Look, I'd better get going."

Someone tapped on the back door. I groaned inside – Sean's face was hovering on the other side of the glass.

CHAPTER NINETEEN

Mom opened the door.

"Oh, hi. Sorry. Wasn't really snooping," Sean said.

Harmon looked over his shoulder. "What's up?"

"I was about to make scrambled eggs, but you'd vanished. Followed your footsteps," Sean said.

"Quite the little bloodhound, eh, kid?" Harmon grinned. "Smells great in here."

"You're too late," I said.

Mom waved him in. "Shut the door. We're already freezing."

Harmon muttered, "That's my fault, too. I want to use the old radiators, but those damn heating guys are trying to talk me into forced air, which would mean a complete overhaul of the system. I can't afford it."

"We're okay," Mom reassured him. "As long as you keep the rent low. This place must have been in a pretty sorry state, eh?"

"Yeah. I don't know how Lotta kept herself warm. The furnace was ancient. But I'm pretty sure she just used a few rooms. The mold and mildew was awful everywhere except for your living room – which was her bedroom – and the one that Addy calls the studio. The rest of the house was a rabbit's warren of moldering boxes and papers and junk."

Sean butted in. "Sounds like a real weirdo. A hermit, right, Pop?"

Harmon considered him for a moment, then said, "*Weirdo* might be too harsh, but she was certainly *different*."

"But she hid away in the house for years and years, right?" said Sean.

"Yes, she did kind of hide away. There was some sort of family tragedy or something. Mrs. Grimes had moved away when she got married and didn't come back for a number of years so she wasn't sure what happened. But she seemed to think that it was this, er, event that sent Lotta completely over the edge."

"What happened?" I demanded. "Did her family die?"

Harmon looked at me. "What makes you think that? I don't know if anyone died. Mrs. Grimes only said there was a sort of family tragedy."

Sean laughed. "Addy's got the whole scenario figured out. Hey, you could be a newspaper reporter. They take all sorts of dramatic license."

I glared at him. "Shut up!"

Sean held up his hands. "Oooh, very intense."

"You're an idiot!"

Harmon looked at each of us in turn. "Hey, you two! You'd think you were brother and sister."

"I'd rather die than have him as a brother!"

"Jeez, relax, will you," Sean said. "It's not like you knew the lady or anything."

He was right. Why was I feeling so angry and defensive? Then I realized it was the terrible sadness I'd heard in Lotta's voice during the argument in the studio. Had I really heard any of it? It all seemed so real. And what about my dream? Could a dream describe a past event? Was any of it possible? If so, what had happened to Lotta's family? What was Freddy supposed to warn them about?

"She must have lived a very lonely life here all those years." Harmon's voice broke into my thoughts. "No husband, no children, no ... love. So little happiness."

"Maybe she didn't want to be happy," I muttered.

"What do you mean?" Harmon asked.

"Yeah," Sean said. "What would stop someone from at least trying to be happy?"

"Maybe she was afraid to."

"You've lost me, Addy," Harmon said.

"Sometimes it's easier not to try ... not to hope for happiness. It'll just get taken away, so what's the point?"

Mom said gently, "That's a very pessimistic view of life, Addy."

"Just trying to figure out why she hid away like that, Mom," I lied quickly, but her eyes were worried.

Fortunately Harmon distracted her. "I do know Lotta ended up in a mental hospital for a while. Mrs. Grimes didn't know for how long – but, well, this is all secondhand, so who knows what's accurate and what isn't?"

"She really *was* in a mental hospital. She *was* crazy." I could hardly breathe. "That's what Freddy said –"

"Freddy?" Harmon asked. "Who's Freddy?"

"I – I mean Page. Yes, Page. She told me about it."

"Page? How would she know about it?"

I shrugged. "Well, maybe it was someone else."

"You'll ace language arts. Writing fiction," Sean said grinning. "So how come you aren't going to Kelvin?"

Mom frowned. "Addy's taking home studies for a while. She's been ill." She clapped her hands together. "Hey, you guys gotta go. I'm due at work."

Harmon grabbed his sweater and hustled Sean out the back door.

"Hey, Addy, I've never met Victor," Sean called. "Can I come up later and see him? He sounds amazing. Take it easy, Pop, don't shove. I'll end up splattered all over that nice white snow!"

Harmon grinned at us. "Just ignore him, Addy. He's too nosy for his own good. Get down those stairs, kid, and make me another breakfast." As he was closing the door, he looked at Mom. "Take some time, Jill, before – well, see you later, huh?"

She nodded.

What was that all about?

Then she turned to me, and in her serious Mother-Voice said, "Addy, sit down. We need to talk."

My heart sunk to my knees. I braced myself.

"Don't worry," she said. "I'm not going back on our deal. This is about your dad."

"I told you I'd call him and tell him what I – we've decided. I promised I'd do it and I'll *do* it."

"I've already talked to him," Mom said.

"You did? About school and stuff? Is that what you meant about Dad thinking you'd made a big mistake? When did you call him?"

"Last night. When I got home. Well, after Sharon left. She came over after work. She said some things that made me realize I'd better talk to him. He wasn't pleased about being woken up so late, either."

"I can't believe you talked to him! You promised –"

"I know, I know. But I needed someone else – not Sharon, not Harmon – to talk to ... and, well, your dad made up my mind for me."

My mouth was dry. "You just said you *hadn't* changed your mind!"

"And I haven't. Your dad doesn't think home studies will work ... with good reason. I agreed with a lot he had to say ... until he started picking up steam and lecturing me – and then I got mad. Anyway, it was very ... intense."

"But you didn't change your mind?" I tried to keep the panic out of my voice.

"No. I've told you that! You see, I *know* you, Addy. Sharon doesn't. And your dad hasn't been here to see how sick you were. So, for now, things will go on as you and I planned. But just for *one* term. Then we talk again.

Okay? However, I still want you to speak to your dad. He has some good points to make."

"He shouldn't have a say in anything I do!"

"He should and does have a say. He's your dad. He just doesn't happen to agree with me on this one, that's all." She straightened her shoulders. "But I'm here, so I'm the one who has to make the important decisions." She glanced at her watch. "I've got to get going. Six people are waiting for me. We're starting tomorrow on that film about North End women. I'll take an early lunch and pick up your school stuff Monday, okay? Can you make dinner tonight?"

"Huh? Yeah. Okay." I was still sorting out what she'd said about Dad. "What should I make?"

"My recipe for parmesan chicken is on the counter. Make a salad and throw some potatoes in the oven around four thirty."

She rummaged in the closet by the kitchen door and pulled out her goose-down coat. "It's probably too early for this, but I've been so *cold* since we came here. I'll call later, Addy. Make sure you answer, okay? Have a good day." She added with a tight smile, "Schoolwork starts soon, so you may as well enjoy your last few hours of freedom."

Chapter Twenty

On Tuesday morning, before she left for work, Mom said, "Did I tell you that I saw Sean last night? Did he try to visit again yesterday?"

I nodded, studying my new French book with great intensity. "I was too busy, so I just ignored him. Besides I'd already fed Victor." I didn't tell her I'd had a movie marathon all day — including one of my top ten, *Bell, Book and Candle*. If I was a witch like Kim Novak, I'd turn Sean into a package of sunflower seeds and feed the whole pile to Victor.

"He asked himself up for coffee last night, too, and I had to tell him it was too late." She laughed. "I think you have an admirer."

I rolled my eyes and moaned. "Mother, please, give me a break." But for some reason, as I said it, I felt lighter … strangely pleased. Why? Wasn't I "in hate" with the guy?

"You'll probably see more of him when you go to school next term. I think he's in your grade."

My rising spirits dropped with a thud. "Why do you keep going on about next term?" I cried. "I hardly started this one!"

"You'd better get used to the idea. You *are* going back to school after Christmas, Addy."

"Just give it a rest, okay? *Okay?*" Panicky feelings I hadn't had for two days made my stomach lurch.

"Right. Well I've got to go. Are you going to be okay all day alone in the house?"

"Absolutely," I announced fervently.

Mom had brought my new schoolwork home the day before. The people at the correspondence office arranged for me to work on the same semester courses as Kelvin High – math, French and language arts. It looked like more work than I'd ever had in real school.

As soon as she left, I raced through bed-making and dishes and threw a load of laundry into the tiny washing machine in the kitchen. Then I got to work planning a calendar of assignments and due dates.

At about ten thirty, someone knocked on the door. Josh stood alone on the other side of the peephole. I was about to open the door when he banged on it with his fist. I stepped back.

"Hey, Addy!" he called. "I gotta get that guitar off you. Page needs it!"

I didn't move a hair. Had Page really sent him? He pounded the door harder. "Hey! Give me the goddamned guitar, kid. I gotta take it to Page!" Then he lowered his voice and said, "Hey, kid, I know you're in there – I can hear you breathing. Just go get the damn guitar, okay?"

I tried not to breathe. Page wouldn't send him to get the guitar. He wasn't going to get it from me – even if I was barely upright on jellied legs. Finally, after a couple more bashes on the door, I heard another voice shout something. Josh let out an incoherent growl and pounded back up the stairs. A few seconds later, Harmon knocked.

"You okay, Addy?" he called, but I didn't answer. He waited a few seconds, then said, "It's okay, kiddo. I'll talk to you later."

I felt like a fool not letting him in, but what if Josh was listening and came back down after Harmon left? I couldn't concentrate after that, so I sat by the window and stared outside. Half an hour later, Josh strode down the front walk, climbed into his rusty van, and drove off with squealing tires. Not long afterward, there was a soft tapping at the door. I looked through the peephole then opened the door cautiously. Page's face was pale, her eyes red.

She smiled tremulously. "Thanks for not giving my guitar to him."

"That guy's a creep!"

"He's short of cash, that's all. Can I come in for a second?"

"No. Wait there – I'll get it."

"No! You have to keep it! Please."

I stared at her. "He knows I have it. He'll kick my door in."

"No, he doesn't know you have it, Addy. He was just guessing. Really. He won't come back."

"Why do you stay with him?"

She pulled her sleeves down with the palms of her hands and wrapped her arms around her chest. Her smile was a wistful fleeting thing. "He's got no one else. He has a bit of a temper –"

"A *bit?*" I tried to laugh but couldn't pull it off.

"But he's really sweet most of the time, you know?" she continued, as if I hadn't spoken. "He's stuck by me through ... everything. We're a team. He's —"

I held up my hands. "It doesn't matter. I don't really care. But if he comes back here, I'll give him the guitar."

In a tiny voice she said, "He won't be back. Honest. You wanna come out for a cup of coffee or something? I was going to walk over to that little place on the corner and —"

"No. I — I'm busy. I have something ... something on the stove." And I closed the door in her face.

After that, I made myself concentrate on the French articles *le* and *la* and past perfect tense, whatever that was. The sun came out and the room was warm and quiet, falling into that mid-morning lull when time seems to stand still. I got a lot of work done, and around noon I had just made myself half a toasted cheese sandwich when I heard a loud squawk from across the hall. Victor.

I gathered up the little pile of apples and carrots I'd prepared for him and went next door.

"Hello, my baby, hello, my honey —" Victor sang. "Play with me, stay with me!"

I ignored him and opened the blind. The room became instantly cheerful and warm — almost as if it too was trying to entice me. But I couldn't give in. I dropped the food into his feeders and scuttled out to catcalls and loud raspberries from the little brat in the cage.

Later that afternoon Page came back again, but I didn't answer. I heard her call out "Addy? Can we talk?" but I ignored her. She'd try to make me do something I didn't want to do ... something I couldn't – like go to the club tonight.

If only people would leave me alone.

I tried working on my new cross-stitch kit in the late afternoon, but it was so dull and ugly and boring that I threw it in the garbage. I wanted to do something really beautiful.

I thought about Lotta's fine stitches and how she'd blended them so perfectly. It was weird, as if the tree tapestry, with its little scenes, and the half-finished angel, and then my dream about the paper-winged woman with her glowing threads had all infected my brain. I couldn't seem to stop seeing colors all around me. I watched the late afternoon sun change the snowy outside from variations on cream and gray and brown to a deep gold, with splashes of brighter color from people's woolly hats and scarves – apple red, pumpkin orange, Popsicle green.

Even the way the buttery light hit a jug of flowers that Mom had on her desk – Lotta would probably have used many different shades of green, yellow and gold thread to get the right mix of pale and dark leaves. I really *really* wanted to work on one of her patterns. But I couldn't ... not yet, not searching through her stuff in that room.

On Thursday, Page was running down the stairs when I was on my way to feed Victor. I was surprised at how happy I was to see her.

"Hi!"

Startled, she looked up, gave me a quick wave, and kept going. Why did I feel such a letdown when she didn't stop and talk to me? I'd been the one avoiding *her*. And why was she wearing sunglasses in the house? Was that a bruise near her right eyebrow? No … probably just too much makeup.

When I got back into my apartment, with Victor's pleas for company still echoing in my head, the phone rang. I didn't answer. It rang a few more times during the day. It was probably Dad, and because I wouldn't have the nerve to hang up on him again, I didn't answer.

That night Mom came home with an old answering machine she'd borrowed from someone at work. "Why don't you ever pick up the damn phone!"

I shrugged. "I'm not ready to talk to Dad yet."

She growled. "But *I'd* like to get through to you some-times, you know! Besides, you've got to talk to him soon. We'll phone him after dinner."

"I'll call him when I'm ready."

She shot back, "You'll call him when I tell you to call him, missy. He's blaming *me* now – saying I'm keeping you from talking to him! Enough is enough, Addy! Are you listening?"

"Yes. I am listening. Okay?"

"Okay! Now, let's eat."

I followed her meekly down the hall.

She was quiet at dinner and I was happy to have no lectures. She didn't even comment on the canned soup and ham sandwiches I'd thrown together. As we did the dishes, I noticed there were dark smudges under her eyes. She sighed each time she lowered something into the soapy water.

"You okay, Mom?" I asked.

"Yeah. Fine. Are you? Are you getting out for walks?"

I bristled. "I've been too busy – getting all my work organized and ... you know."

She rubbed the dish mop over a soup bowl again and again as if trying to rub off the pattern. "You'd tell me if there was anything *really* upsetting you ... wouldn't you? I think with the move here – all the changes ... I was wondering if a therapist might help you." One glance at my face and she said, "Never mind, don't get worked up. I'm too tired to go through all that again. Look, let's call your dad and get it over with."

The knot in my stomach squeezed tighter. "Do I have to? Right now?"

Her face hardened. "Yes. Living room. Now."

With that, she turned on her heel, marched down the hall, making a big theatrical deal of it, demanding I sit on the couch and wait while she dialed. I almost laughed out loud when she finally had to admit that Dad wasn't home.

She slammed down the receiver. "You can take that smug little smile off your face, Addy. You *will* talk to him."

We tried to watch TV for a while, but Mom may as well have been a mannequin in a store window for all the attention she was paying. Most of the time she stared out the window, then she said in a chilly tone, "I'm tired, Addy. I need to go to bed. Do you mind?"

Mom slept on the pull out couch in the living room, so I didn't have much choice. I mumbled good night and trailed down the hall. She hadn't even lifted her face for a kiss. I hated it when she got all cold and withdrawn. I could try to make her come around – by apologizing for something, like I usually did. I had enough things to choose from. I'm sorry I won't go to school. I'm sorry I won't talk to Dad. I'm sorry I laughed at you when he didn't answer. I'm sorry I'm such a loser. I'm sorry I'm such a wash-out as a daughter.

I turned back toward the living room but stopped when I heard a snuffling sound. Mom was curled up on the couch, her head turned away, her shoulders shaking. I wanted to tell her … I almost did. But instead I ran to my dark room and threw myself on the bed.

Chapter Twenty-one

The next morning, Mom stood in the kitchen putting her coat on, looking as if she hadn't slept.

"I *would* have talked to Dad last night," I said, fiddling with a crust of toast.

"You'll get your chance tonight."

"Please don't be mad, Mom."

"I'm not mad. We need to talk after I get home, okay?" She sighed. "I *am* worried, Addy. I've made three attempts to get you to go out lately and you had an excuse every time. I'm worried –"

I cut her off. "I've just had too much to do. I'll go out later."

Mom looked at me speculatively. "You're sure?"

I tried to laugh. "Of course. It's not exactly fun being alone all day."

"And that worries me, too, Addy. You're alone too much."

I couldn't look at her. If I told her the truth, she'd force me Out There – with cheerleader cries of 'You can do it! Go get 'em, Tiger!'

"You're making a big deal out of nothing," I said. "I'm fine."

For a few seconds she was silent, then she nodded, "Okay. I'll do a big shopping on my way home tomorrow, but we need a few things today. I made a list." She took a piece of paper out of her pocket and pushed it across the table.

I stared at the list. "You want me to go to the store?"

"Yes. It's not far. It'll get you out for a bit. Is that a problem?"

"No. No problem," I said, my eyes still on the tiny slip of paper.

Mom put her hand over mine. "Dress up warm. Do you know the way to the store? If you have any problems —"

I pulled my hand away. "What problems? Jeez! I'm not five years old."

Mom's face sagged. "I'd better get a move on."

She quietly left the room, carrying her boots. I trailed behind, wanting to make things better again, and even though the thought of going Out There had wiped out my appetite, I said, "Want me to make baking-powder biscuits for the stew that's thawing?"

"It doesn't matter," Mom said, that weary edge still in her voice. "I'll see you later, okay? Call if … never mind — you know where I am."

"Mom?" I said, as the door began to close behind her.

"Yes?" Her head and one shoulder appeared.

"I'm — have a good day."

She smiled wryly. "Sorry I'm so touchy, sweetheart. You have a good day. And don't forget, we're calling your dad again tonight."

"Okay, Grandma. Yes, Grandma." I answered with our favorite joke, except it didn't feel funny.

When the door clicked shut, I swallowed back tears. This was so stupid. I could try out for a daytime soap soon. Cry-at-the-drop-of-a-hat Addy. I'd got what I wanted, hadn't I? No more school. Free to stay home. Free to stay in the house. Except for going to that *damn* store. Except that I knew for sure Mom was closing in on me.

I went to my room, put on jeans and a heavy sweater, then dug out my winter jacket and boots. Mom said Nucci's opened at eight thirty. It was almost that now. Maybe there wouldn't be many people in the store this early.

I walked on stiff legs to the living-room window and looked down at the street. Directly below me, Josh and Page were walking away from the house. He had his arm around her shoulder. A stab of jealousy sliced right through me. Page had everything and I had nothing. I *was* nothing. But then Page shrugged off his arm, and for just an instant, Josh turned to look at her, his face tight with fury.

Page moved ahead of him, but his hand shot out, grabbed the sleeve of her jacket and spun her around. At the same time, Page turned her face up to my window. She said something and he released his hold, but not before giving her a little shove. She waved up at me, and I lifted my hand in return. As they walked away, Josh put his arm around Page's shoulder again. This time she didn't push it away.

What was that all about? Whatever it was, they'd worked it out quickly. They were so lucky to have each other.

I had no one.

A few minutes later, I stood at our apartment door, my hand hovering over the doorknob. Mom would expect those groceries on the kitchen table when she got home.

I had to do it.

With two cloth bags in hand, I carefully locked the apartment door behind me. I expected to hear Victor, but only silence met me in the hall. Probably sulking. I clumped down the stairs. When the front door swung open under my mittened hand, a wash of cold damp air took my breath away. On the road, cars splashed by through the wet snow. A woman walked past the gate, pulling a red-cheeked kid in a blue sleigh. I could hear its gliders scraping on the pavement beneath the snow. Along our walk there were three sets of melting footprints – Mom's, Page's and Josh's.

I could do it, too.

Couldn't I?

My warm boot sunk deep in the fresh snow. At the same time, my lungs shrunk to the size of snowballs. I couldn't take a deep breath, just short gasps.

Through the blood pounding in my ears, I thought I heard someone whisper, "Don't go out there. Stay with me."

I stumbled backward, closed the door, and leaned against the staircase banister. I lowered myself onto the bottom step, my knees creaking like the Tin Man's. If only I didn't have a heart – then it wouldn't be banging around in my chest.

I had to go Out There. I had to! If I didn't, I'd end up completely nuts – just like Lotta Engel.

I stood up, determined. I took one step forward and the solid door seemed to shift and waver under a faint, shimmering light. Once again, a distant voice sighed, "Don't go."

I bolted – straight up the stairs.

CHAPTER TWENTY-TWO

I sat on the floor in the hallway for ages, staring at my apartment door. I knew if I went through it, I'd have failed. I needed some time to think – to prepare. I had Victor's key next to my own. Should I? What if I heard more voices? But I had to go in there, really. It *was* my job to open things up in the morning and I was late already. In a weird sort of way, I wanted to hear Victor talk – to be sure that the sounds were coming from a living being – even if it was a shabby gray bird.

The studio door creaked open. The room was as gloomy as a cave except for thin stripes of light that lay over the worktable like yellow threads.

"That you? That you, my beauty?" The cage shifted under its cloth dome. "Can't breathe in here. Lights out! Lights out!"

When I pulled off the cover, Victor opened his thick yellow bill and wrapped it around one of the brass bars. I checked his food and water. He still had lots. His head lolled sideways and one beady eye looked up at me coyly. "I looove you," he said around the bar. "Looove you maaadly! Staying today? Play with Victor?"

I sniggered. It was crazy, but I was sure he was grinning back at me.

"It's your lucky day, Victor."

In a quavery girlish tone, he began to sing, "It's a long way down on this roller coaster ... the last-chance streetcar ... went off the track ... and you're on it. Tell me, tell me what's the matter, Mary Jaaayne."

"You know Alanis Morissette?" I laughed. "Boy, my music *must* be loud. You have ears like a hawk, even though you look more like a scruffy little vulture."

He climbed up the side of the cage and hung upside down, his head twisting to keep one bright eye on me. "Please be honest, Mary Jane ... are you happy ... please don't censen yer beers," he crooned.

"That's *censor your tears*. But not bad, Victor. In fact, downright weird," I muttered. "You sound just like her."

He walked back down the bars and onto a swinging perch. "More bruises –" He moaned. "Tell me, tell me what's the matter, Mary Paaage."

"Mary Jane, not Mary Page! I *am* nuts, talking to you."

"Baaby, don't hurt me like thaaaat!" he muttered, then turned away from me.

I made a face at his chewed-up red tail and hunched gray back and walked to Lotta's worktable. The white sheet over the unfinished canvas looked ghostly in the wan light. I pulled it off and sucked in my breath. Someone had definitely been working on it. There were dark blue threads mixed into the gray of the wings, and now there were more reddish accents here and there, too, like splotches of blood. Below the angel's skirts, the swirling darkness was broken by a small pale hand reaching up, as if trying to grab the floating fabric. The canvas below the hand was bare. Who belonged to that hand? The effect was so grim, I wanted the creature to turn around – I needed to see its face. I leaned closer and once again the stitches dissolved before my eyes, leaving behind bare canvas.

I braced myself, ready to hear voices, but only the muffled sounds of honking cars and the neighbor's barking dog could be heard in the distance. Well, at least this time I was only *seeing* things. Definitely an improvement. On the table beside me was a selection of silks and a small pincushion shaped like a pear, spiked with half a dozen needles. The threads were the same – dull blood red, navy blue, pale cream – that had vanished from the canvas. I hadn't noticed them laid out like this when I was in here before.

I stared at the unfinished angel. Could I ever create anything even half as amazing as this creature was going to be – dark and frightening as it was? *Going to be?* Wrong. This tapestry would never be finished.

I studied the remaining stitches. They were so carefully placed and blended that the finished part of the feathers looked almost real. If I used that blue just where the feathers overlapped, it would smooth out their raggedy look and they would stand out even more. But what if I chose a brighter, lighter color. Would that make the picture less grim? Maybe teal blue or silver?

A soft sigh slid past my ear, followed by a tut-tut sound, as if someone was clicking their tongue against their teeth. Victor. That bird may be only a foot high, but he was definitely flesh-creeping at times. Another slow drawn-out sigh, so close I could almost feel my hair move. A cold chill shivered through me. I grabbed the venetian blind cord and gave it a hard yank – uncovering the whole window.

"Yipe!" Victor croaked. "Lighten up, baby, lighten up the skies, eh? Throw some light on the subject. The subject is dead! Dead but not gone."

"Shut up, Victor!" I called out. He let out a short sharp humph and glared at me.

In the clear warm sunlight, my eyes took in the dusty shelves, the specially built cubicles stuffed with colored yarns and thread, rolls of fabric, plastic and wooden boxes filled with little cardboard squares, each spun round with colored silks – pale pink, deep red, shimmering blues, greens, yellows, soft grays and earthy browns – embroidery hoops and little ceramic pots stuffed with paintbrushes and felt markers and pencils. Here and there gauzy cobwebs trailed throughout.

Glancing outside the window, I was startled to see many of the same colors repeated there – the sky had at least five different blues in it this morning and Harmon's tiny herb garden sticking out of the snow was made up of – gosh – dozens of browns and greens. Even purple and pink. Was this how Lotta saw the world? In shapes and colors?

I started to sort boxes. Suddenly I knew I had to clean the room up – get it ready. It didn't matter why, a voice inside me said firmly. It just had to be done.

I took off my jacket and dusted and organized everything near the worktable until I came to an open rolltop desk piled high with bolts of canvas. When I moved them aside, I saw that the desk was stuffed with papers, ledgers and letters. Lined along the top of the desk were six books, each one with the same author's name printed on its spine.

Lotta Engel.

Curious, I pulled one out. Its cover was a glossy photograph of a tabletop casually spread with all kinds of sewing paraphernalia. The title was *Lotta Engel's Advanced Needlepoint.* She'd had a book published – no – six books! *Lotta Engel's Needlework for Beginners, Lotta Engel's Best Designs, Crewel Embroidery by Lotta Engel* and a nearly identical pair, *A History of Tapestry and Needlework – Volume One* and *Volume Two.* How had she published six books stuck away in this house?

I flipped to the first book jacket flap and saw the head and shoulders of the dark-haired girl. The features were older – with a slight hollowness around the cheeks and eyes. The lips, finely formed, were thin, the bottom one firmly compressed. The type under the picture read "One of the world's foremost experts on needlework, Lotta Engel has been sewing since she was thirteen years old.

She lives in the prairie city of Winnipeg, Canada. Her magical, otherworldly designs are sought by collectors all over the world."

I pushed an assortment of junk off the swivel chair in front of the desk and sat down. I checked the date of publication. 1977. Before I was born. Lotta Engel ... the recluse ... she wasn't just some nut who sewed to keep herself from going mad? I checked the publication date on the two history books. 1987. Much later. Did her neighbors know she was 'one of the world's foremost' *anything?* Harmon mustn't know either! Hadn't bothered to check out this desk. Too busy with wonky furnaces. How had she managed it all? Through letters? She sure had a huge pile of correspondence crammed into her desk.

I lifted aside a ledger. Underneath was a letter that lay open, as if it had just been read. The date was March fifth of this year. Only seven months ago. The letterhead was in pale blue – Griffin Fine Arts Gallery.

Dear Miss Engel,

Thank you for allowing me to visit you at home. I hope that you will consider my offer to have a show of your work this year. It has been many years since Lotta Engel's work has been on display. I had read about your Angel Series (they have taken on an almost mythical existence!) and was thrilled to be able to see and touch a few. I know you are reluctant to show your work these days, but it would be exciting for Lotta Engel collectors and admirers to see this series of amazing pieces executed during your early years. I hope your latest piece is going well. I would have loved to have seen it, but I understand your reluctance, as it is unfinished. Once again, may I assure you that the Angel Series would be the highlight of Griffin Gallery's year. As I also mentioned, we would frame the pieces for exhibition, so you need have no concern on that score. I hope to hear from you soon, regarding this exhibition and any of your more recent works.

Yours very cordially,
Myra Todd Mechen

So, some gallery was trying to get her to show her angel tapestries. Did she agree to do it? I remembered her words to Freddy: "'Make friends with the angels, who, though invisible, are always with you.' That's what I used to believe. But I don't believe anymore, Freddy. They've turned their backs on me. I can't hear them."

If all the other angel pictures were done many years ago, before ... whatever happened to her family and before her time in a mental home, would she agree to show them? Somehow I didn't think so. Had she even answered the letter?

I got my answer right away. Underneath the gallery letter was a sheet of mauve paper with a few lines written on it in black spiky handwriting.

Dear Myra Todd Mechen,

After some consideration I have decided to allow you to

hang my Angel designs, including my latest. It will take some time for me to finish it, but I would like it hung with the others, as I feel it completes the cycle of my life in many ways. I cannot promise you a date. I will write to you when I draw closer to the final few stitches. I don't have much time left, so if I cannot manage to finish, perhaps someone would be kind enough to

I turned it over. Nothing on the other side. Why had she stopped?

She had decided to do it – to show her angels. The letter didn't have a date, so I couldn't tell when she'd written it. I felt a cold chill move across my forehead when I once again read "I don't have much time left." What did she mean? That her *own time* was limited?

Had she known she was going to die? Had she planned it?

I looked at the unfinished angel as it swirled away into the silky night. 'Gone so far away that I can't hear them anymore.' It would always remain a half-formed, raggedy-looking creature in a gloomy sky.

This wasn't my room. These weren't my letters. I shouldn't be here. I must have said it out loud, because Victor cried, "Stay with me. Don't go! We all alone. Staaay!"

We? He and I? Did he have any real idea of what he was saying? Even if he didn't, he was right. We were alone.

Why not stay?

I could make it my own quiet place. I'd tell Harmon about the letters and books and the tapestries, and he could decide what to do with them. I wouldn't have to make the decision. Just wrap up the angels, push them aside, and ignore them until he dealt with them.

Victor continued to mutter away. I caught the words "Get it done" and "silly girl must stay," but I tuned out his jabbering and surveyed the room.

If I shoved the dining-room table against the wall and spread the chairs around, I could clear a space straight through to the armchair and the fireplace. To avoid delving deeper into Lotta's life, I pulled the rolltop down on the desk, piled the bigger boxes in front of it, then slid the framed tapestries on top.

I pushed and pulled furniture until I was practically seeing double. Soon, I began to feel less like an invader. Victor certainly seemed to approve, offering tidbits of idiotic advice like "Dust to dust and under the rug. Get to work, finish it up." He banged around in his cage, hanging from his perch, tossing seed shells and bits of carrot onto the floor, and preening and marching and acting stupid — all the time fixing one bright eye on me.

When I stood back to look at the results of all my labor, it wasn't perfect, but I liked it. It had been fun to poke through cupboards stuffed with packets of needles, little spools of glittery and plain threads, and all kinds of scissors — some very old and shaped like birds and animals — and a whole drawer full of embroidered pincushions, trimmed with seed pearls and twisted ribbons and clearly too old to be anything other than a special collection. There were still a couple of drawers to sort through, but

I had lots of time to do it slowly.

The part I liked best was the alcove beside the little fireplace, where I'd created a cozy sitting area. A place to study, and maybe even sew.

A nasty little voice inside me whispered, *Yeah, until you hear Lotta and Freddy again,* but I shook it off. The whole room felt warm and friendly. I was strangely calm and serene inside. Something I hadn't felt for ages. I stood over the design of the unfinished angel, itching to sew on it. It was almost as if it was calling to me to finish it. But how could I? I'd only ruin it.

I turned back to the worktable. Square in the middle of the worn scrubbed surface was a book – *Lotta Engel's Needlework for Beginners.* I must have put it there when I was looking through her desk. Settling down on a straight-backed wooden chair and leaning my elbows on the table, I started to read.

Before long, I was eager to sew. Maybe just one tiny section … I picked up the selection of colors laid out beside the unfinished winged creature and examined them one by one. I even threaded a strand of the dull red into a blunt-tipped needle and pushed the needle into one of the tiny holes in the creature's wing. Instantly I felt a faint electrical buzz pass into my wrist along with a deep, almost painful, yearning – and at the same time a feeling of well-being and peace.

But then I pulled the thread right through.

I couldn't do it. What if I wrecked it? Even though I'd

done a dozen small pictures and I knew I was capable of neat stitches, did I have the right to touch this incredible piece of work?

Not yet.

A loud snort of disgust behind me. I put the needle and thread back into the pincushion and said out loud, "I can't."

"Go ahead, go ahead!" screeched Victor. "Be my number one. Be my only one. You're the only one."

"It's not mine to do, okay? I wouldn't know how to finish it properly even if I wanted to." I hit my head with the heel of my palm. "What am I doing? I am making excuses to a *bird,* for pete's sake. It'll be a straitjacket next."

"You're a cracker-jacket!" he cried. "You're the one. Do it for me, honey-lamb. Do it for Lotta."

"Do it for Lotta?" I whispered.

He banged around his cage, cackling like mad. Suddenly it dawned on me. Victor had belonged to Lotta — Harmon said she'd probably talked to him all the time. So, he was probably only repeating the things she'd said to him over the years — *in her voice*. It was Victor who'd spoken the other night, mimicking two people he'd heard so long ago.

"Man, you had me going, Victor," I said, relief making me laugh giddily.

He just glared at me as if simply lost for words.

I turned back to the table. I'd filled a shoe box with scrap stuff as I'd cleaned up — small pieces of penelope canvas, bits of thread, a couple of loose needles. I took out a piece of canvas about the size of a small envelope. Then

I opened Lotta's sampler page and chose the tiny design of a small blue flower she called 'Forget-me-not.'

I taped the edges of the canvas to prevent it from unravelling, then slowly, carefully, began to sew, centering the design as she advised, counting stitches as I went. Periwinkle blue, dark green, corn-silk yellow … I didn't want to use her good stuff – not yet – and by sorting bits of scrap threads carefully, I found enough variety to perhaps finish the tiny design.

I decided to use a silvery thread on the edge of a petal, and when I put in the final few stitches, a soft gasp fluttered past my ear. I held the flower at arm's length. The silvery blue was perfect, giving the tiny flower a thin splash of light that made it come alive.

"You'll do," said a woman's deep voice. "You see? You'll do just fine."

I stiffened. "Wh-hat? Who …"

The voice continued, as if instructing a pupil. "Nicely done. Tight. Even. Good eye for color. I was right. You *will* do nicely."

A spray of sunflower seeds hit my arm and soft curved feathers drifted past my face. Victor clattered his bill through the bars and cackled, "Good girl! My pearl, my girl. Don't you leave me now! Not forget me. *Forget-me-not.*"

I glared at him. "You are very, very spooky, Victor, but you won't spook me anymore." He made a loud kissing sound, and I picked up a few of the scattered seeds and threw them back at him, laughing.

My stomach rumbled. I was actually hungry – really hungry. I glanced at my watch. No, it couldn't be. Two o'clock? I'd been here for over five hours?

Mom would be home in less than three and I hadn't cleaned up the apartment – and then there was dinner.

Dinner. Groceries. *Going Out There.*

My appetite vanished, just like that.

With damp fingers, I packed up my sewing, then slowly dragged on my jacket. I told myself that going to the store wasn't the same as spending hours in that horrible school. It couldn't be.

I could do it.

"See you, Victor," I said, my voice tight.

When I opened the door, the woman's voice said, "Don't go. Please."

I turned and said, "I'll come back as soon as I can. I promise."

And the weird thing was I meant it.

CHAPTER TWENTY-THREE

I stood at the open front door, holding my breath. "Take one step," I muttered. "Just one foot after the other. *You can do it.*"

"Snow too much for you?" a voice said right beside my ear. "Hey, wait. Don't go running off again, okay?"

I stopped, one foot on the first stair.

"Man, you're like a scared rabbit or something. One word, and you're *ssssmokin'!*" Sean stood, hands on hips, in jeans and a gray sweatshirt and bare feet, his hair wet.

"Jim Carrey you will never be," I said. "And I am *not* scared." Much.

"You've hurt me to the quick," he said, one hand over his heart. "So what are you doing? You were going out and … changed your mind?"

"Yes. I – I forgot … I'm not feeling well."

He laughed. "You forgot you weren't feeling well?" He reached over and shut the door. "Forget a lot of things, eh?"

I started up the stairs.

"Hey, Addy, come on. Don't get all high-horsey on me. Pop says I've got a gargantuan mouth, and I know a few more who would agree. I humbly beg your forgiveness."

I looked at my mittened hand on the stair railing. I knew I was posed like a distraught starlet in a bad movie, but I couldn't move.

"So, where were you going when you remembered you were feeling sick?"

"To Nucci's. I have to get stuff for dinner." I looked at the closed door and a fist tightened around my guts. "I – I guess I'll try later. Maybe ..."

"I could go for you," he offered. "I have to get some soft drinks and chips anyway. Old Herbal Harry in there won't buy them on principle. He says it's like putting acid in a car's gas tank."

"And it is," said a deep voice from the doorway.

Harmon grinned at me. "Where you been, kiddo? Feels like I haven't seen you for weeks. As soon as I kick this lazy bum out, we can have the cookies I just baked – oatmeal raisin."

Sean grinned. "Ah, sugar. Acid for the old tank, eh?"

When Harmon clapped Sean's shoulder with a massive hand, Sean winced and pretended to sink under its weight. "He's off to school Monday, Addy," Harmon said, "and none too soon either. His papers finally got transferred. And no more pub visits either – getting in everyone's hair. I'm not able to do a thing with him loafing around."

Sean grinned. "As a matter of fact, I have an urgent job to do myself, Pop. I'm off to the store – for the maiden in distress. Honest. Any junk food that comes back here will be strictly coincidental." He stuck his hand out. "You got a list? And money?"

"Well, I wasn't going to rob the place," I said, digging in my pocket with heady relief. I folded the list and put it into my change purse, which Sean stuffed into one of my cloth shopping bags.

"Hey, a joke, she actually made a joke," Sean said. "There's so much untapped potential, eh, Pop?"

"Ha, ha," I said lamely, but couldn't help smiling.

"I'll call you – no, you don't answer your phone. I'll knock on your door when I – no, you don't answer the door, either. Just how would you like this delivered, ma'am?"

"I'll answer my doorbell. Don't worry," I said. "Two long and three short – that's the signal."

"Another joke. The girl's killing me!"

Harmon grabbed his ear and walked him to the door. "Just bring it home. She'll probably be eating *sugar* down here. Get going."

"You guys have to wait for me." With that Sean shoved his feet into a pair of Harmon's enormous duck boots by the door, grabbed his jacket off the hook, and was gone.

"Ah, there's my timer going. You want to come in?" Harmon asked.

"I promised Mom I'd clean up," I said. "I'll come down in a bit." I started up the stairs, my feet light. The way I felt right now, I bet I could go Out There soon. I smiled when I thought about Sean. Maybe I didn't actually hate him after all.

I had barely made the beds and cleaned the bathtub when my buzzer rang. Sean must have flown to the store and back. Why didn't he use his key, the idiot! I ran down the stairs and swung the front door open, expecting to see Sean's silly grin. So I didn't quite get what I was seeing at first. The man standing on the front step was familiar. But he was in the wrong place.

"Dad?"

CHAPTER TWENTY-FOUR

"**M**e. In the flesh."

Dad was smiling, but his eyes were weary and his thick gray-blond hair stood up on end. "The cabby kept getting lost. How can anyone possibly get lost in a city with one main street? And snow in October! Well? Can I come in?"

I stepped back. "Yeah. Sorry. I'm just —"

"Surprised?" He stamped snow off his shiny brown shoes. "Your mother has managed to make me so crazy, I had to come. Look at you. Skin and bone." He hoisted his carry-on bag higher onto his shoulder. "Do I get a hug or are you still not talking to me?"

I threw myself at him. "I'm so glad you've come, Dad. We'll do great now."

He pried my arms free. "This is just a quick visit, Addy. Now that you're feeling better, we'll get you back home, eh?"

He wasn't here to stay.

"But let's deal with all that later, Addy." Dad pulled me in again for a tight hug. "It's so good to see you, kiddo. Lead the way to your — seems weird to say it — but to *your place.* I need a cup of coffee."

He followed me up the stairs. "God, Addy. Do you think your mother could have found more of a dump if she'd tried?"

I saw the stairway through his eyes: the stained wallpaper, the thin carpet, the chipped and peeling paint on the banister.

"That's because I'm still working on the place," said a voice from below. "I'm Addy's landlord, Harmon Wenzer. I heard a strange voice – just thought I'd make sure she was okay."

Dad frowned down at Harmon, taking in his red muscle shirt, gray sweats and leather thongs – and his bulky muscles bulging and flexing as he wiped his hands on a dish towel.

"I'm Addy's dad, Walter Jarrick."

Harmon said, "Well, hi there, Walter! I've just made fresh coffee and cookies, if you and Addy would like some. After you've freshened up a bit."

Dad's face stiffened. "I don't think so. I've just flown in. Excuse us."

Harmon held up one hand. "The door will be open, and the coffee's on –"

"If you'll excuse us?" Dad repeated, nudging me between the shoulder blades. "I'm dead on my feet."

"Okey-dokey," Harmon called out. "See you later, Addy."

"Dad!" I whispered, when we reached the landing, "you didn't have to treat him like that."

"Muscle-bound bonehead. Probably illiterate from the look of him." Before I could argue, he added, "I don't like

161

you hanging around with weirdos. What the devil can your mother be thinking of —"

I hissed furiously at him, "Harmon's a nice guy. He got Mom that second job and —"

"Okay, okay, relax." Dad followed me into the apartment, dropped his case by the door, then looked into each of the rooms. In the kitchen, he stared out the back window, shaking his head. "It's even worse than I imagined. This isn't an apartment — it's a poky little hole, and it's cold as hell in here. No wonder you've been sick."

"I forgot to turn up the heat this morning —" I began, but he yanked open the fridge door.

"There's nothing in here. She always was irresponsible, but this is ridiculous."

I hadn't seen him for almost three months and he'd turned into a through-and-through stranger.

"Tomorrow is our big shopping day," I said. "I've lost weight because I've been sick. Tonight we're having stew and biscuits and …"

But he wasn't listening. He was opening drawers and cupboards and slamming them shut one after the other.

"It's Mother Hubbard's bloody cupboard. What's she been doing with the money I've been sending?"

He marched down the hall again and stopped in the middle of the living room. "I see a bathroom, kitchen and your room. Where does your mother sleep?"

I pointed at the couch. "It pulls out."

Dad rolled his eyes. "From a three-bathroom, four-bedroom house to this – and what's this about a second job? This Harmon character got her some kind of work?"

"Yeah. Want to go downstairs and really meet him? He's –"

"*Tea and cookies* with that sumo wrestler? I don't think so! I'm going to take a rest on your mother's ... *bed* here. You can start packing."

"Packing?" I stared at him.

"She can freeze in this dump and live on cheap stew, but my daughter isn't going to –"

"Dad. I'm not leaving. I'm enrolled in correspondence –"

"And that's another thing I intend to put a stop to." He threw his jacket over Mom's office chair and loosened his tie. "What a balls-up she's made of things. Well, it's over. She can –"

"You didn't come to see how I was, did you?" I cried. "You came to prove that Mom was messing up. Well, I'm not going anywhere."

"Addy, you're still under age. I have – in that briefcase – a lawyer's document that gives me the right to –"

"I don't care what you have!" I shouted. "I'm not going with you! I'm not going *out there*. I'm not!" I stalked away from him.

"Stop right where you are," Dad growled. "If you go down to Bluto's apartment, I'll be right behind you. Now I've got to use your bathroom. Don't move."

He walked quickly down the hall again. Threads of anger shot along every nerve ending in my body. I was out the door in a flash, but halfway down the stairway, I hesitated. Sean would be back soon and Dad would storm around and make a scene and embarrass me to death. But I couldn't stay in the flat and let him put an end to everything that Mom and I had worked out together.

When the distant rush of water flushed in the apartment, I unlocked the studio door and slipped in.

CHAPTER TWENTY-FIVE

"Trouble's a-brewin'. Up and down and all around," Victor growled, pushing his beak through the bars and snapping it a couple of times.

I put one finger to my lips. "Shhhh. Be quiet!"

"Be quiet yourself, my little flower," he whispered back. "Shhhh. Shhhush. Trouble all around. He'll come. Cut me into little parrot pieces. Carrot parrot pieces."

"I'll cut you up into parrot pieces if you don't shut up! How did Lotta put up with you?"

He said in a sad little voice, "She was not refined. She was not unrefined. She was the kind who keeps a parrot. À la Mark Twain."

"Victor, you're a feathered encyclopedia!"

He stared at me silently, his head to one side. I was sure he was frowning. I laughed. "Gotcha! You don't know what an encyclopedia is, do you?"

"Tick a lock. Get back to work! Both of you!"

I laughed again. He looked so funny, all ruffled and angry. "What kind of work am I supposed to do? And no one else is here, silly. So just shut up."

He turned his back on me. "Shut up, Victor." He made little sobbing sounds. "Poor Victor Parrot. Poor little Victor." He fell silent.

"Sorry, old fella," I said. "Blame my father. He's here trying to force me to go away with him."

Victor perked up. "No go! Girl stay!"

"Don't worry, I'm not going anywhere. Relax."

If only *I* could.

I'd have to face Dad sometime. I glanced over at the worktable, longing to read more of Lotta's book. Darn. I'd forgotten to cover up the half-finished angel again. Even *I* knew you had to keep the work free of bright sunlight and dust.

I hesitated. What if I saw those same phantom stitches that melted away? I closed my eyes and then opened them quickly. The canvas looked exactly as I'd left it – even the needle with the dull red thread was stuck in the pincushion nearby. For some reason, I felt disappointed.

A low muttering came from Victor's cage, as if he was talking to someone in a hurried whisper. Then he began to pump up and down, his ragged tail and head bobbing. Seeds flew and more carrot bits hit the floor. "She can do it. Get her to help! Get her to help!" he shrieked.

"You okay, Victor?" I asked, walking cautiously toward the cage.

Looking over his shoulder, he said in the woman's voice, "There's no one else, Addy. I have to stay, don't you see? And you have to stay to finish it."

The light shifted, bounced off the brass birdcage and fluttered across the carpet like broken sunlight. Then, for a split second, I saw a woman's head with straight black hair and bangs, and beneath them, deeply shadowed eyes. Two white hands appeared, lifted and moved toward me. I stepped back with a cry, and the light shattered and fell. But not before I heard a voice say, "I'm so tired of being alone. You will help me – I know ..."

My hair crawled across my scalp. "Help you do what?" I squeaked. "Work on the angel? Is – is that it?"

"That's it and more. Much more. Much more than this," Victor began to sing, bouncing around his cage. "I did it myyyy waaaay!"

"This is insane!" I cried.

"Says who?"

I spun around with a little yelp.

Sean stood in the doorway, a grin on his face, Mom's bulging shopping bags in his hands. "So this is spooky old Victor? Why are you yelling at him?"

"What are you doing here?" I demanded.

"Your father is downstairs. Pop told him that you probably went to the store. By the way, you owe me two bucks. Didn't give me enough."

"Is my dad angry?"

"The idea that you were out shopping seemed to settle him. So I snuck away and came looking. They don't call me Gumshoe Sean for nothing."

"Are you sure they don't call you Creeping Charlie?

You'd better go."

Victor tossed some seeds at him, shouting, "Yeah! Yeah! Go away, 'kay? Like, take a hike, maaan."

Sean parked the grocery bags beside the door and swaggered over to him, pretending to draw imaginary pistols. "Are you talking to me? Are *you* talking to *me?*"

"Shut up, both of you," I snarled. "I don't want my dad to hear us."

"So why are you hiding from your old man?" Sean asked.

"That's none of your business."

"Yeah, bub!" Victor sneered. "You never listen, Page. Well, I'll make you listen."

"Shut *up,* Victor!" I snapped.

He glared at me. "Bad girl! Baaad girl!"

Sean laughed. "Pop says your dad lives in Toronto, but your parents aren't divorced yet, right?"

"And they're not going to be." Who was I kidding? The old anxiety crept into my stomach like threads of ice.

"Divorce isn't so bad. Or at least it wasn't for me until my mom married that jerk. I could tell she was secretly relieved when I left."

"And Harmon?"

"Pop? He's cool."

"Does he want you here?"

"Like I said, he's cool." Sean wandered over to the angel canvas. "So what is this? Yours?"

It really bugged me that he seemed so unconcerned that his parents weren't together anymore. I picked up the white cloth from the floor and covered the canvas. "No."

"Get to work!" Victor shrieked.

"Shut up, Victor!"

"Lotta says shut up — all say shut up," Victor moaned. "Poor Victor. No one love him. But I looove Victor."

"Well, there's a needle and thread laid out," said Sean. "Sure you're not working on it?"

"I wouldn't know what to do. There's no pattern. Even if she told —"

"Who? Page?"

He was so close I couldn't catch my breath. I stepped out of the way, pretending to search through the book for something. I flipped open a page with a parrot on it — gray with a red tail — sitting on a branch in a thick jungly tree. She'd used Victor as a model. No one else had that clear unearthly stare.

"Hey! It's crazy old Victor, " Sean said.

I snatched the book out of his hands. "He's not crazy."

"Yeah, bub. He not crazy-daisy! Bub!" came my echo with a spray of sunflower seeds. "You do what I say, Page. Or else!"

"Hey, Victor. Relax. And I'm not Page. She isn't here," Sean said. "That's the second time he's called her name."

"He must hear Josh and Page upstairs. We can hear them sometimes, too, but we usually have music or the TV on."

"So what's this?" Sean was leaning over the picture loosely wrapped in black cloth on the pile in front of the desk. I reached for it, but he'd already flipped open the cover.

"This is neat. Little scenes about a family or some-thing, it looks like. And what's this? A burning car?"

I leaned over his shoulder to look where he was pointing at the red sky behind the girl bent over her needlework. He was right. A small car was engulfed in flames, so carefully stitched that it seemed to blend into the crimson sky.

My fingertips tingled. I knew instantly what it meant – my dream – the sounds of the engine roaring and the crash of metal. That's how her family had died. She'd asked Freddy to warn them because she *knew* they were in danger. He didn't warn them, and they had died. All of them. Her mother, father … the girl with the blond curls and the smiling boy, Eli. The gravestones were theirs, the ones she was sewing in the picture.

"Her brain was definitely tilted a bit, eh?" Sean said.

I pushed him aside and tied the picture up tightly with its colored threads. My hands were shaking. I wanted to cry for Lotta and her family. It was so awful. Poor, poor Lotta.

I had to get a grip. I had to.

"Man, are you tense or what? Tense and intense."

Victor called out, "Tense, intense, build a fence, *don't fence me iiin!*"

Sean laughed. "I hate to tell you this, buddy, but you are majorly fenced in." He looked at me. "You too, eh? Hey, you okay? What's up?"

"Nothing," I said sharply.

"So how come you don't go to school like regular people?"

"I just don't, okay?" Why was he asking so many questions? Why didn't he just go?

"But how did you manage it? I suggested Pop let me stay home, but he wouldn't touch it." He said it so nonchalantly. School was nothing to him. How could he imagine what it was like to be terrified to go? What would he think of me if he knew? "Now my marks and stuff are here, I've gotta go. So how *come* you aren't going? You don't seem sick anymore."

"God, give it up, okay?" I snarled. "You wouldn't get it! Just leave me alone about school!"

He grinned. "Man, you really are the Princess of the Great Huff. And here I thought we were getting to be –"

"Just get lost!"

"I *could* go down and tell your dad where you are," he said sweetly.

"Go ahead!"

He grimaced. "Forget it. Why help him out? My dad's worried, I can tell. I think he's afraid you and your mom will leave with your dad."

"So what if we did?"

"From the way he talks, he's kind of sweet on both of you. But especially your mom. All he does is –"

I glared. "You spew more garbage than Victor!"

"Yeah, bub! Garbage. Spew, spew! Shut your trap! Or I'll shut it for you!"

Two dark red stains melted across Sean's cheeks. He put his hands in his pockets and nodded. "Garbage-mouth *Bub,* that's me."

He turned and walked slowly away, head down. My anger dropped a few notches.

Victor, sensing victory, stuck his beak out of the cage. "Here's your hat, what's your hurry! Ha!"

I rolled my eyes. "You can cut the act, Sean. It would take more than me to upset you." I couldn't believe it – I'd never talked to a boy like this before.

He looked over his shoulder. "Yeah? Like you know me, huh? Creeping, Garbage-mouth, Gumshoe, Big-mouth Wenzer?"

"So, what are you telling me," I asked, "that you're actually a Sensitive New-age Guy?"

"A what? Hey, yeah ... that's the real me. *New age. Sensitive.*" He threw out his arms and spun in a circle.

I laughed. I couldn't help it. It was weird. My emotions were all over the place.

He ran his hand over his hair, brushing it forward. "Look, I'm sorry. Pop warned me to go easy. I just thought you needed a bit of cheering up. Considering."

"Considering what?"

"Well, all you've been through ... today and ..."

"Just what exactly has he told you?" I demanded, feeling the smile drop off my face.

Victor leaned closer to the bars, glared at Sean and snarled, "Trouble, trouble. Take off, bub. Or I'll make you, see?"

Sean and I said simultaneously, "Shut up, Victor!"

I glared at Sean. "Well?"

He held up both hands. "Pop didn't say much, honest. Just that you've been sick and that you get ... well, upset easily – that you get panic attacks or something."

"I do not!" I said through gritted teeth. "Your father should keep his nose out of my life!"

Victor stamped up and down his perch. "Hit the deck, bub! Hit the deck!"

"Hey, I'm sorry, Addy. I just thought –"

"Maybe that's your whole problem. Maybe you should give up *thinking* because you seriously stink at it ... maybe ... maybe you should just *drop dead!*" I banged through the door.

And slammed right into Page.

CHAPTER TWENTY-SIX

Her books fell with a thud and a pile of papers floated around us. I bent to gather them up, muttering "Sorry, sorry" and shoving them at her. I felt like my brain was about to explode.

"No problem. Maybe by mixing up all the pages, you've actually organized my essay, eh?" Page stuffed the papers back inside their folder, then peered behind me. "Hi, Sean. How come you're not at school?"

"I wish I was. I'm in trouble here," he muttered.

"Yeaaah! Big trouble!" piped Victor.

Page pushed past Sean into the studio, dragging me with her, the sleeve of my sweater pinched between her fingers. Sean tried to follow but I glared at him. Giving me a quirky smile, he backed out of the room and closed the door. I felt instantly guilty.

"I just bought some blackberry tea," Page said, "wanna come up to my place?" She looked tired, her skin so pale I could almost see through it. And there definitely was the skim of a greenish-yellow bruise above her right eye. I hadn't imagined it.

If I went upstairs with her, I'd avoid Dad – maybe long enough for Mom to get home and sort things out. If possible. I needed time to breathe. To calm down inside. "Tea sounds great."

"Victor get tea, too. Two for tea and tea for two." Suddenly his crackly voice changed, became deep and gruff. "You'll do as I say, Page!"

Page grabbed Victor's cage cover and dropped it over him. "We hear him talking gibberish all the time through the old heat vent." She pointed to a metal grate in the ceiling. "I'm worried that Josh is going to do him in."

"Red alert! Red alert! Goin' down. Goin' down!" came a muffled voice from under the cover.

A jolt of alarm shot through me. "Josh wouldn't really hurt him, would he?"

Her voice was weary. "No, no, of course he wouldn't. But that idiot bird keeps shouting back everything Josh says. It's driving Josh nuts."

I said quickly, "Maybe I could take Victor for safe-keeping in my place."

"What about your mom?"

"She'd be okay I think. I'd have to check first."

Victor said in a deep growl, "I love you, baaybeee! You listen to me!"

Page said quickly, "Let's go. But talk to your mom, okay? Before he ends up as Parrot Fricassee."

Victor let out a long high shriek. Page and I laughed and suddenly I felt a lot better.

I took the two grocery bags and followed her up the stairs. There was a small landing, its walls covered in a collage of music posters. Inside, the gabled room was a mess – clothes and junk everywhere – and it reeked of cigarette smoke. A scattering of shabby furniture stood around a small brick fireplace and old woven rug. In one corner of the room was a makeshift kitchen, with dishes piled high in the sink.

Page sat down on the couch and untied her boots. They thumped on the floor. "I know – it's a pigsty. Josh's stuff is tickety-boo perfect, but he won't lift a hand to tidy up anything else. He never lets up on me, though." She rested her head on the back of the couch and closed her eyes. The pale bruise went right down the lid and into the lashes.

I sat on the edge of a plastic chair. "How'd you hurt your eye?"

She touched it with her fingertips. "Banged into the corner of a kitchen cupboard. Stupid, huh?" She got up and plugged in the kettle. "So I noticed you cleaned up Lotta's room. You using her stuff?"

"Just a few threads and that. To try out. I – I probably won't use anything much."

She opened a package of tea and spooned some into a red teapot. "You should."

"Did you know Lotta Engel was really famous once?"

"I don't know anything about her, except what Harmon told me. Famous, huh? For what?"

"She published six books on needlework, and on one of the jackets it says her artwork was collected all over the world. And there was a letter on her desk from an art gallery practically begging her to show her stuff. She was writing them back, but she didn't finish the letter. It wasn't that long ago, either. I looked at a bunch of her tapestries. They're strange, but really beautiful."

"Well, who'd a thought, huh? I'd like to see them sometime. Did you tell Harmon?" She handed me a cup of something that smelled like sweetgrass. Didn't anybody drink normal tea in this house?

"Not yet. But I will." I chewed my lip, then added, "My dad's just arrived. I'm hiding out from him."

She frowned. "Are you afraid of him?"

"Oh no! He thinks Mom's made a big mistake coming here and wants me to go home with him. Back to Toronto."

"And will you?"

I couldn't very well say, 'I can't go because I'm too scared to walk to the end of the street, never mind enter an airport,' so I said, "I can't leave Mom."

"Don't let anyone push you around, Addy," she said fiercely. "No one."

Taken aback by her vehemence, I muttered, "I – I won't."

We were quiet for a while. She sat cross-legged on the couch and sipped her tea. Then we just sort of fell into talking. I could feel myself slowly relaxing inside. She told me about university, and I told her about my new schoolwork and then we came back around to Lotta's books, and I told her how I'd read the first chapter and had sewn the little flower.

"She has this half-finished piece on a frame that's a mix of embroidery and needlepoint. It's an angel with its back to you. You're going to think I'm crazy, but every time I look at it, I want to finish it for her. It's kind of like ... I have to, you know?"

Page looked at me. "So why don't you?"

"I – I couldn't. It wouldn't be right."

"But it isn't so much the work that's important, Addy, it's the *design*. I bet she'd have loved to see it finished. I would, if it was mine and I'd died. At least I think I would."

"You see? You're not sure. I don't know what she planned for all those empty areas. The angel is floating in a very dark night sky. It's pretty depressing – and right now the figure almost disappears into the background. I'm sure she'd want it to stand out. I thought maybe a bit of lighter blue and green where the light would shine on the feathers, but ... I couldn't make a decision like that for someone else."

"Wait!" Page ran to a cupboard, rummaged in it, and waved a large piece of folded paper in the air.

CHAPTER TWENTY-SEVEN

Page spread the paper on the couch. "I was storing stuff in some boxes that Harmon gave me the other day and this was in the bottom of one. I put it aside to give it back to him. As soon as you mentioned an angel in a dark sky, I knew right away what it was."

I looked at the design, carefully painted onto a sheet of graph paper. The angel's wings seemed to flow and blend into the night sky, which swirled around it. Why were these colors so different from the rich vibrancy of her earlier angel pictures? The way these dark whirlpools moved around the angel, it was clear that it was rapidly moving away, into a kind of murky nothingness, its back toward us.

Below the creature was a distorted and tangled landscape with twisted trees writhing into the sky, and through that turmoil, another small figure was tumbling downward, one arm reaching up, the pale hand trying to touch the angel's skirts. It was a girl, with long black hair coiling through the night sky. As I looked at it, I felt a strange, thrilling excitement. Was that Lotta? What did it mean?

Maybe I *should* change the colors – make it brighter, less grim looking. Maybe I could move the girl – have her standing safely on the ground instead of caught forever trying to reach that dark angel.

Could I? Should I do it?

"I wonder why the angel isn't facing us," Page said. "And that girl … why doesn't it see her?"

I replied softly, "I think the angel's forgotten her."

Page sighed. "I can get into that. Gramps always said he'd be my guardian angel when he died. So, like … where *is* he? I need someone to … talk to." She gave me a tight smile. "Silly, huh? Never mind, I have you to talk to. You have this, like, inner strength – kinda makes me feel – I don't know – better somehow."

I couldn't help it. I let out a whoop of laughter. "Inner strength? Me? That's a good one."

"You know what? Your whole face changes when you smile. You should do it more often," Page said, folding up the design and handing it to me. "Oh now, don't go all long-faced on me again! You're much better looking when you're animated."

"When I'm what?"

"Really interested in something. Like this angel design. I hope you don't mind me saying this … and don't get mad," she said, holding up her hand, "but I see this really fierce look on your face sometimes. I know you're dealing with something really hard. That's when I see the strength inside you – fighting. Don't go getting that prickly porcupine look, Addy. I've had lots of times when I've been unhappy – or scared. And the crazy thing is, most of the time I don't know why I'm so miserable!" Her laugh was sad and a little bitter. "And then, sometimes I do. You know what I mean?"

"How can anyone be strong and scared at the same time?" I blurted out. "It's impossible!"

"No, it's not. Even strong people need help now and again, Addy – when the fight gets too big for them. You know ... there are people who can listen, who can help."

"No one can help. You don't understand – how could you – you have everything."

"I do?" Her face was open with amazement.

I stood up. "I've gotta go."

"Addy ... please don't be mad," she said. "Everyone is getting mad at me these days. I have such a big mouth – we can talk about it – I'll explain –"

"You don't have to. You're talking about a shrink. I'm not a mental case." I held out the pattern with shaking fingers. "Here. I don't want it."

"Of course you're not a mental case!" she exclaimed, ignoring the pattern. "Lots of people go to shrinks. I do."

"You do?"

"Yeah. At the university. I just started. One of my profs advised me to go," she said, then she shrugged. "Anyway, I've been twice. I like this doctor – she's really nice, even though I'm not sure I agree with everything she's telling me."

"But you don't need a shrink!"

"Why not? You don't have to be a drooling lunatic to need someone to talk to, Addy. If you want, maybe she'd see you – or give you the name of someone else who's good."

"I don't think so," I said, turning away. That voice

chimed again and again in my head. *You'd have to go Out There. You'd have to go Out There.*

"But, Addy ..."

"What part of *no* don't you understand?" My voice was hard and dry in my throat. I had to get away. But Dad was waiting downstairs. I was trapped.

"Addy, I'm sorry, don't —"

The door banged open and Josh strode into the room. "Wasting time as usual, eh, Page? You should have come to rehearsal. It's all falling apart. That little shit Tom never showed up. Why am I the only one working his ass off!" He banged his fist on the wall so hard, I felt as if he'd hit me. I took a step back and bumped into a chair.

The whole room vibrated with something that scared me cold.

"I've — I've got to go," I croaked.

Josh ignored me. "Have you been telling that little jerk to miss rehearsals, Page?"

"Of course not! I told him off myself yesterday. Tom doesn't listen to anyone."

"How did you see him yesterday?" he shouted. "Are you two meeting behind my back?"

"We met on campus, by chance. He's thinking of taking a music course at night."

Another thump on the wall with his fist, a stream of foul words, and I skittered past him. As I ran down the stairs, I knew I was leaving Page alone with a crazy man. I knew I should go back up and see if she was okay, but, coward that I was, I kept right on going.

CHAPTER TWENTY-EIGHT

"Addy!" Dad stood halfway up the staircase. "Where have you been?"

I stopped dead – I'd left the stupid shopping bags on Page's living-room floor. I slid the pattern under the studio door and slammed through the doorway into my apartment. I couldn't save Page. And I couldn't face Dad.

Coward! Coward! Coward!

I threw myself on the bed. Everything was a tumbling, seething mess inside my head – Josh's rage, Page's white-lipped acceptance, my argument with Sean, Dad's sudden arrival and demands that I pack my bags. What would Mom say when she got home and found him here? And – oh jeez – how was I going to get those stupid, stupid groceries? Stupid Sean Wenzer – why didn't he just leave them with Harmon like he was told? Why did he have to come upstairs and find me? Why did I go up to Page's? If I'd just gone to the store myself, like I was supposed to, most of this wouldn't have happened.

"Addy?" Dad called softly through the door. "Don't cry, kiddo. I'm sorry this has started out so badly. Look, can we talk? Can I come in?"

"Just a minute!" I wiped tears off my cheeks and opened the door a crack. "I was going to have a nap. Mom likes me to rest before dinner."

That sounded lame even to me, but he bought it. Just as well, as the fear was eating its way back into my head, my throat swollen with more tears.

"Okay, sweetie." His worried face hovered on the other side of the door. "You rest while I heat up the stew for dinner. I've got your groceries. Some girl from the upstairs apartment said you left them in her place. White hair and a pierced nose! What a bunch of misfits. What were you doing up there?"

Misfits? I wanted to shout at him – like your crazy loony daughter? Instead, I muttered, "I'll make dinner later."

"You want to talk for a bit, then?"

He looked really upset and I knew I'd probably never sleep now. I was about to give in when he added, "We've got to sort out this mess, Addy. I'd like to talk to you without your mother coaching you on what to say. I think we should –"

I couldn't believe it. He was doing it again. "I do have a mind of my own, you know." I closed the door in his face.

Flopping down on the comforter, I stuffed Biddy behind my head and tried to breathe slowly and calmly. The afternoon light was fading. The wind shook the tree outside my window. Puffs of wet snow slopped against the panes, leaving wet snail trails down the glass. Tears drizzled into my hair and ears. All the time tears. My head felt stuffed, like Biddy's – but with noises and people and skittery images that I couldn't seem to slow down. I tried to think of something else.

Lotta's tree, with the burning car and the solitary young woman sewing away on the gruesome gravestones, floated past my inner vision. What dark world had she lived in after the death of her family? Harmon said she'd lived many years alone in this house. All of those fantastic, colorful angel pictures that the gallery had wanted she'd made before the tragedy. And she hadn't sewn angels for years afterward. So, why had she started on the last angel picture just before her death?

Had she really become a sad and lonely recluse? Maybe not. Maybe she'd been perfectly happy alone in this house with her sewing. Maybe she had the right idea – just stay away from people and lead a nice peaceful life, relying on yourself.

Maybe she had turned *her* back on the angels.

I could understand someone like that. The last few days in the apartment, working on my schoolwork, not answering the door, had been so peaceful. Free of hassle all day long. It's only when people got involved that things turned messy and horrible. Sean poking his nose in where it wasn't wanted. Page. Josh. And there was still Dad to deal with. Lotta had been right to stay away from people. That way she couldn't disappoint anyone. Not even herself.

I pulled an afghan over my legs. The soft pat-pat of snow on the window and the swish of cars grew distant ...

I was sitting in the studio looking at the angel. I could use the dark green and red mix and then, where the wings curved around the angel's back, I could change it to two strands of dark gray mixed with one of viridian. The tips also needed another hue of red worked through them.

What was that? Someone knocking on the door. Maybe it was my order from England – those silks I'd been expecting. I had just reached the top of the stairs when the air around my head was filled with the loud flapping of wings. Suddenly the steps dissolved under my feet. Freezing air swooshed past my face. What was that terrible sound? Something was crashing down the stairs.

I found myself standing on a ledge outside a window. I could see the studio behind me, but the window was covered with a thick slab of glass. I spread my fingers over it – cold as ice. The unfinished angel seemed to flutter on the sewing frame.

I would never finish it now.

There were sets of stairs all around, leading toward the blackness above and the streets below. But they all began about ten feet from the ledge. I could never jump that far. Not Out There. A cold wind blew around my legs. I knew that if I could just let go, I would be able to fly to safety – to a luminescent green expanse I could just make out hovering above the ground – past the yard and beyond the neighboring streets. I knew it was a beautiful place, filled with wondrous things – like white Bengal tigers, songbirds, parrots and exotic flowers. I wanted to go, but I couldn't.

At that moment, a voice right behind me screeched, "It wasn't me! Leap! Leap to a conclusion. A leap in the dark! It wasn't my fault!"

Suddenly I was surrounded once more by the loud whapping and fluttering of wings. My fingertips scrabbled across the glass window behind me, but I couldn't get a grip. Something pushed me hard between my shoulder blades. Air rushed into my throat and blocked my scream for help. I banged against each stair tread on my way down, down, down.

CHAPTER TWENTY-NINE

"Addy? You okay, sweetie?" Mom gently pushed the wet bangs off my forehead.

"I was on a ledge outside the house and someone pushed me off." I shivered. "At least I think it was me. But I felt like someone else. She — I was falling and I couldn't stop myself —" I stopped, my eyes widening. Was that how she'd died? Falling down the stairs?

"Never mind," Mom's voice broke in, warm and soothing. "You're back now. Safe and sound."

"Yeah ... safe and sound," I muttered, then I sat up. "Dad?"

She smiled. "I know ... your dad's here."

My legs and arms felt as if weights were attached to them.

"I'm glad you went to the store, Addy. I saw the grocery bags."

"I'll take a shower," I said, struggling to get up.

"Plenty of time for that. Your dad and I want to speak to you first, okay?"

"He's talked you into something, hasn't he?"

"No, no. We've just … *talked*."

"I'm not going back to Toronto, Mom."

I can't go Out There. I can't!

She nodded. "No one's going to make you do anything you don't want to do. Okay? We'll just chat."

I dragged behind her down the hall, dreading the *chat* and still a bit dazed from my dream. In the past few days I'd had a couple that felt as if they were actually happening. I remembered the flap of wings, the push against my back, and Victor crying, "It wasn't me. Leap! Leap in the dark!"

Had he deliberately pushed me … Lotta?

"Ahh, here you are, kiddo."

The dream faded next to the reality of my father sitting on the couch in new jeans and a denim shirt. He was holding a full wineglass and trying to look casual and cool, one ankle on the other knee, his penny-loafered foot jiggling in the air. Would Addy Jarrick's real dad please stand up? The Dad I knew didn't like wine, and he'd always sneered at middle-aged men in jeans, saying they'd never grown up.

"Sit down, honey," he said. "Your mom and I have been talking."

I perched on the edge of Mom's office chair.

A look passed between them. I clenched my hands into tight balls. Dad leaned forward and placed his glass carefully on the coffee table. "Look, Addy, your mom and I –"

At that moment, someone rapped on the door. Mom got up. Dad rolled his eyes. "Just leave it, Jill."

"I can't. The only people who knock live in this house. It could be important." She walked quickly out of the room and came back followed by Harmon, dressed all in black with a blue and white dotted bandanna tied around his head like a sweatband.

"I was heading to the club early, so I thought I'd offer you a berth before I went," he said to Dad.

"A what?" Dad was looking at the bandanna as if it might unwrap itself and spit at him.

"A place to crash. Jill's pretty cramped up here."

Mom smiled at him uneasily. "That's really nice of you, Harmon — I was wondering how we'd arrange it —"

Dad stood up and hitched his jeans over his paunch. "What do you mean — *wondering how we'd arrange it?* I came to visit my family, Mr. Wenzer, and I don't think we need you to organize our sleeping arrangements."

"Wally!" Mom said. "Harmon was only thinking of your comfort —"

"I believe your friend Harmon was thinking about something other than my comfort, Jill," Dad snarled. His neck was deeply flushed above the crisp collar.

"Hey, relax," Harmon said. "I've brought up an old folding cot. It's on the landing. But I have a much better bed in my spare room. My son, Sean, can use the couch. Your choice, man. I don't want to make waves."

Dad snorted. "No waves here, *man.*"

Mom looked stricken with embarrassment. I wanted the floor to swallow me up. Why was Dad being so utterly horrible? He'd slept in the spare room the last few weeks we were in Toronto anyway, so what was he making such a big deal about?

"Thanks, Harmon. I'll let you know. Just leave the cot. It was really nice of you," Mom said, putting her hand on Harmon's arm.

That's when I understood. Had I been blind? Even Sean had hinted at it. Harmon liked Mom. More than just a friend. When he gazed at her, like now, his face was soft, and there was a look there – one I'd never seen on Dad's face – a look that said Harmon Wenzer would fight dragons for Jill Jarrick. Mom's flushed face gave nothing away. She didn't even make eye contact with Harmon, but there was an electricity between them that was as strong as a power surge.

Harmon gave Mom a warm smile, then turned the beam on me. "Okay, Addy?"

"Fine," I said coldly. "He *is* my father."

"Which you seem to forget, *Harmon,*" Dad said, emphasizing his name with a sneer. "If you don't mind, we're having a family meeting here."

"Right. Sean's making his version of spaghetti carbonara – it could get scary – then I've got to push off to work."

Mom glared at Dad and followed Harmon out. Dad paced in front of the window, glancing down the hall now and again. "He actually goes to work dressed like that? God, the guy's a joke. He's a bouncer, right? Time to grow up, I'd say. I can't *imagine* what his kid is like."

Mom stood in the doorway. "Harmon is very grown-up, Wally. And for your information, he's half owner in the pub and his son is perfectly normal. By the way, I have to go in tomorrow – they're short-staffed. So you and Addy can have time alone."

"And you can have time alone with that gorilla?"

"What I do here is my business," Mom's eyes were wide with warning. "Harmon's been a very good friend to both Addy and me. Right, Addy?"

I stared at her. "I don't know. Maybe."

"Addy! You know it's true."

I shrugged. "He's okay, I guess."

Mom turned to Dad. "And I won't have you accusing me of something I'm not doing, Walter."

I could tell Dad didn't believe her, but he glanced at me and said, "No point in upsetting Addy. I'll put the cot in the kitchen. It's only for a few days. I won't overstay my welcome – if I'm welcome at all."

Mom brushed her hand over her eyes. "Of course you are. And no one's pushing you out, Wally. Let's get back to the important issue here, and that's Addy."

My heart sank into my stomach like a cold stone. Here it comes, I thought. Something they've thought up – something that will force me Out There.

"Addy, sweetie," Mom said, sitting on a footstool near me. "I've told Dad everything that happened ... again." She threw him an accusatory glance. "We both know you're still not well."

"No kidding," I murmured sarcastically. "I've tried to tell you —"

"What your mom means is that we feel that ... *emotionally* you're not well. She says that you seem *afraid* to go outside and that —"

"I'm not afraid to go outside! I haven't gone out because I still feel queasy now and again. That's all."

"Addy," Mom said quietly, "did you go to Nucci's for those groceries?"

"Why are you asking me that! Did Sean tell you —" I could feel the panic starting under my ribs.

"No, but Harmon said —"

"Harmon told you I didn't go to the store?" I couldn't believe it — he'd blabbed to Mom. The panic slid aside, and a cold flame of anger took its place.

Mom pulled me down beside her. "He didn't tell me anything. He just handed me a can of plum tomatoes and said that he thought Sean — then he changed it to *Addy* — forgot to buy one. He'd double-checked the list. Did Sean go to the store for you? Is that what happened, Addy? *Are* you afraid to go outside? Is that it?"

My cheeks were burning hot. My anger turned into a surge of rage that ran down my arms and pooled in my hands. I wanted to hit someone — something.

Dad leaned toward me. "Addy ... did this Sean kid go to the store for you?"

I stood up and began to pace, back and forth and then in circles. I wasn't going Out There. They couldn't make me. My voice shook when I said, "So what if he did? I wasn't feeling well. I was going to go. I was halfway down the walk. He came out, said he was going to the store anyway, so I let him take my list. So what? I was going to go. I was!" I hit my hip with a balled fist.

"Addy! Don't do that. Just tell us the *truth!*"

I shouted, "You want the truth? Okay, fine. You're right. I *can't* leave this house. *I can't leave it.* Are you happy? You want to know why? Ha! That's the joke! I don't *know* why. Great, huh? Look at you – gawking with your mouth open. I couldn't – I couldn't tell you because I'm a freak! Because I'm crazy!" It didn't matter if they knew. Nothing mattered anymore.

"Addy. Please. Listen to me," Mom said, taking my hand and holding it tightly. "You are not crazy. Your dad and I think you may have an illness – it's called agoraphobia."

I pulled my hand away. "Agora– what? What's that?"

"It's a fancy word for being afraid to leave the safety of your home."

"There's a name for it?" I asked, looking at her for the first time.

Mom nodded. "People with agoraphobia have what are called panic attacks if they try to go outside. It's not that uncommon, really. Maybe that's what was wrong with the woman who lived here – Lotta Engel."

"But she was crazy," I cried. "She was in a nuthouse!"

"Listen to me, Addy! I do know one thing for sure. You're *not* crazy. If you're uneasy about leaving the house, we have to find out why you feel this way. I've been testing you a bit, and it seems you'll do just about anything to keep from going outside. Anyway, we'd like to get a doctor in on this – someone who understands agoraphobia and can help you –"

Could it actually be that I wasn't crazy after all?

"But how do you know it's that ... that agora-thing?"

"She doesn't know," Dad said. "She's playing amateur psychologist. But no one believes for one second that you're ... crazy." He turned to Mom. "What have you been saying to her to make her think she's crazy, for God's sake?"

Mom stood up. "Oh no, Walter, you're not going to do this. Not this time. You've blamed me for everything else over the past couple of years, but you won't blame *this* on me!"

"Jill, what the hell are you talking about? You're the one who dragged her here, not me!"

"Why is it you always conveniently forget that you encouraged me to take this job?" Mom cried. "Then you wouldn't leave Toronto."

"You didn't *need* to go anywhere, Jill. You took Addy and now look at what you've done to her – to us."

Mom took a few steps back, as if he'd punched her. "Is that what you believe, Walter? That I –"

I shouted, "It's all about *you* guys, isn't it? I wish I *could* leave this stupid place! I'd be like Page – I'd go and never come back!"

"Addy, please … don't –" Mom started.

I ran out of the apartment and slammed the door behind me. I stood on the landing, expecting the door to open instantaneously. When it didn't, I pressed my ear to it and heard them hollering at each other. Of course, they'd follow me eventually. Now that they knew I couldn't go very far, they could spend all the time they wanted blaming each other for the mess I'd turned into.

Chapter Thirty

"That you, girl?" came a muffled screech from the studio. "Be careful. Don't go!"

Go where? Where did I have to go? I couldn't go upstairs to Page's in case Josh was still there. I couldn't go to Harmon's. I couldn't even go into the studio because I'd left my keys in my stupid bedroom.

I stumbled down the stairs in a fog. Halfway to the main floor, I heard sounds – a grunt and a thump and then furious whispering. When I turned the corner, Josh and Page were standing by the front door. He had her arm pinned behind her back and was talking in a low voice, his face inches from hers. All I heard was "stupid bitch" and "fed up" and then "you'll bloody well do as you're told. I'm sick and tired of you hiding stuff from me. You owe me. Wenzer doesn't even know about these."

Around their feet was a scattering of Lotta's canvases. Page's eyes were screwed up with pain. He shoved her against the wall and pressed his face close to hers, wrenching her arm higher.

Page whimpered, "Addy knows about them. Josh … please."

He spit out, "One more sound and I'll smash your pretty little nose right through your skull. I'll take care of that weird kid. Just do as you're told, understand?"

She nodded, short sharp jerks of her head. Why didn't she scream? Why wasn't she fighting back? Suddenly, he let go of her arm and pulled her away from the wall. Relief washed over her face, mixed with pain and tears. With a quick hard shove, he slammed her once more against the wall. Her forehead hit the plaster, her eyes flew open in surprise, and she fell down hard with a loud thump. Josh stood over her, his hands balled into fists. He raised one booted foot, to kick her.

I don't remember anything after that except a red-hot roar that blasted through my head. It was as if I was outside of myself watching as I threw my whole body against Josh, wrapping one arm around his neck. Thrown off balance, he fell, with me on top of him. My fists banged against his head and shoulders. One part of me was utterly horrified as I hit and hit and hit, using all of my five-foot-nine-inches to cover him with rage, but the other part wanted to beat his head through the floor.

Suddenly I was suspended in the air by my belt, still flailing the air with my fists. Harmon had me in one hand and was holding off Josh with the other. Page was crouched on the floor cradling her arm, mascara running down her cheeks, a red welt on the side of her forehead and down one cheek. Harmon lowered me to the ground. Josh struggled to his feet, and I slithered away from his flailing boot just in time. A fist flew through the air, slamming him against the front door.

"I'll get you for that, you fat pig," Josh whimpered, rubbing his jaw.

"I look forward to it," Harmon said, not even out of breath. "Now get your things and get the hell out of this house and don't come back."

"Piss off," Josh growled.

I gathered myself into a sitting position in time to see Harmon move forward, his face red with fury. Josh bounded up the stairs, coattails flying.

Page was unrecognizable, her features twisted and swollen. "Harmon ... please, make him stay," she sobbed. "He didn't mean it. He'll be sorry when he calms down. He always is. Please."

Harmon shook his head. "No, Page."

Thumps on the stairs and Josh appeared again carrying a duffel bag with stuff hanging out of it. Mom and Dad followed, looking worried. Mom let out a little squeal when she saw me sitting on the floor. My right eye felt hot, my cheek numb.

When Josh yanked open the front door, Page lunged at him, hanging on to his leather jacket. "Josh, wait for me. They don't understand. We'll go to rehearsal."

Josh shook her off. "You *bitch!*" he shouted. The door slammed shut behind him.

"No!" Page tried to run after him, but Harmon grabbed her in a tight hug. She fought him, but she was too weak.

As he led her past me, she pushed her face into mine. "It's all your fault, Addy! I hate you!"

"Page —" I muttered through dry lips.

"He was all I had!"

Dad pushed her away and leaned over me. "My god, Jill, he's given Addy a black eye. What kind of place is this? A bunch of druggies and misfits. *This is it!* No daughter of mine is staying here."

As Mom helped me to my feet, she said something to him I couldn't hear because everyone was talking at once. Sean, needlework canvases clutched to his chest, tried to smile at me, but it kept sliding off his face. Then Harmon said something to Dad, who replied by lunging at him. Mom let go of my arm and tried to pull Dad away, blocking the stairway.

Without thinking, I opened the front door and plunged outside.

CHAPTER THIRTY-ONE

My sneakers slid across a pile of wet leaves and slush, but it was only when my fingers touched the front gate that I realized what I'd done. I'd gone outside. Out There. A sharp pain shot through my head along with a wild surge of panic that gushed up from my toes. When I turned back, I saw a figure standing at the studio window, its hands spread on the glass. I struggled toward the house, but it moved away from me – gathering momentum until it became a glittering far-off speck and disappeared.

A flight of stairs appeared before me. They were made of clear glass and scattered with tattered feathers – gray and black, and one dark red one, like a drop of blood. Through the stairs I could see swirling pewter-colored clouds. I was afraid the staircase would crack under my weight and I'd fall through into nothingness.

Terrified, I crept to the top of the stairs to find a long corridor with many doors, each a different color. I had a single piece of colored thread in my pocket and I knew I had to locate and open the matching door. As I stepped over the threshold the floor dissolved under me, and I began to fall.

"Not again!" I cried. "Oh no, not again! Please, no!"

I woke up, my body jerking, ready for the ground to slam into me. Instead I fell back onto the soft pillows of our couch.

"She should be in the hospital." Dad's voice rumbled in the distance. I opened my eyes.

A stranger with a stethoscope and a small flashlight surfaced in front of my face. He shone the light first into one eye and then the other. "She will be just fine."

Behind him, Mom's face swam into view. "Addy, this is Dr. Mohammed from Docs on Wheels."

"There does not appear to be much wrong," the doctor said to Dad. "Put some ice on that eye and give her a couple of these tablets, and I will check on her tomorrow. I do not like to burden the ER doctors with something that is not an emergency.

"Now. Some questions if you please. How did she get this black eye? I wish to know if the police are required." The doctor had soft dark eyes, salt and pepper hair and an air of utter authority.

Everyone, including Harmon, who was hovering by the living-room door, tried to answer. It was pretty garbled, but I think the doctor finally worked out that I'd come to Page's rescue and the black eye was the result. When he seemed satisfied, Harmon asked him to check Page, too, and they left together.

I sighed and lay back on the couch pillows. Mom bustled out of the living room to get ice and tea to go with the painkillers.

Dad gazed out the window in gloomy silence.

I felt strangely calm. Everyone knew the worst. And I was still alive. I hadn't exploded or died from going Out There. Not this time, anyway.

"I'm very proud of you, Addy," Mom said when she returned, "but please, please call for help next time – if anything like this ever happens again. Okay? You're not exactly Sugar Ray Leonard."

I tried to smile but gasped when a hot stab shot through my face. I pressed the ice pack against it.

"I'm standing here trying to absorb what's happened." Dad's voice was shaking. "You could have been killed, Addy. That creep had a hundred pounds on you." He began to walk back and forth. "I can't figure either of you out. You're living with people who clearly belong to the underbelly of the city."

Mom snorted. "Walter. Come on. That's just paranoid. Page goes to university and sings in a band in a club run by Harmon – who doesn't drink, let alone do drugs. The man's even a vegetarian, for crying out loud. Josh is a disgusting, vicious bully, but Harmon will make sure he doesn't come back. We're perfectly safe here."

"Jill, I want Addy to come home with me. It's not fair for you to have all the control here."

"You want to talk about control?" she hissed. "You've been in control since the day we got married. You're not getting Addy. She stays here."

"I was ready to consider it an hour ago, but –"

I couldn't shout, so I groaned, "Don't – do – this. I'm not a piece of furniture that you can shove around." They began to protest, but I cut them off. "I'm staying, Dad. Page says –"

"*Page* says!" Dad spluttered. "The one being beaten up in the hall? I don't give a damn what someone like that says! You know what *I* think, Jill? I think ..." And he started all over again, going on and on. I finally tuned him out and took the two pills with a gulp of tea.

Mom fussed with my comforter. I couldn't stand it – or the nagging drone of my father's voice. I pushed Mom aside, dragged the comforter off and staggered to my feet. A wave of dizziness made me teeter, but Mom grabbed my arm. Dad followed us down the hall, still letting off a low, steady stream of hostility.

When we got to my room, Mom turned to him and snarled, "Walter, for God's sake! Give it a rest. Look what you're doing to Addy!"

"Wha –"

"At least give *some* thought to what she's been through today."

"Oh ... sorry, kiddo," he murmured. "Sorry."

"Close the door, Walter, please, while I help Addy get undressed."

"Huh? Sure. Okay." He leaned over and kissed me on the forehead. "Addy, I'm just worried about you, you know? I love you very much."

Did he? A swim of tears seared my sore eye. "You're

only going to be here a few days, Dad, and you're blowing it. You're really blowing it."

He looked up at Mom. "I'll go check that stew and we'll talk during dinner. Okay?"

Mom nodded, her fingers pressed against her trembling mouth.

"Dad?"

He turned and looked at me.

"I'm not going back – not yet, anyway. So don't argue about it anymore."

He nodded and tried to smile before walking out, shutting the door gently behind him.

Mom helped me out of my damp clothes and into my pajamas, then sat on the edge of the bed and stroked my hair. "It's getting so long," she murmured. "Soon it will be down to your waist. You want me to cut it sometime?"

"I don't know. Maybe a bit off the ends. Mom?" I hesitated, then said, "About going outside."

"I know, sweetie. I know you can't do it yet. I only wish you'd trusted me enough to tell me. But this move was bad timing. I got so involved in myself and my problems, in work. But I *am* here for you, Addy. You know that."

I nodded. "And I can still do home studies?"

"Of course you can."

My throat was thick with tears, but I whispered, "Mom? Do you think I can really get well? That I'm not ... you know ... crazy?"

She put her cheek against mine and whispered, "You are

definitely not crazy. It will take time for you to get well, but you'll do it – we'll do it together. If you can't go out alone, maybe we can go out for little walks together, just to start with." I stiffened and she sat back. "But only when *you're* ready. And we'll see if we can get someone to come here to talk to you, eh? A psychologist who deals with anxiety and stuff. People with this problem get well … believe me."

"You're sure?"

"I'm positive. Now try to get some sleep."

"Mom?"

She turned, one hand on the light switch.

"I think I knew about Page and Josh – I mean, I think I knew he was hurting her. But I pretended not to notice. Maybe I could have helped her."

"Maybe. But you had enough to worry about, Addy. And next time you think something isn't right, you will do something – like talk to me. We can sort anything out together."

"She was so angry at me."

"It was *not* your fault, honey. She lashed out at you because she needed someone other than him to blame. She has to work it out for herself. Now please … get some rest."

She turned off my light. It was sleeting outside. The streetlights gleamed in rainbows across the wet pavement, reflecting the distorted images of the few cars that drove slowly down the road.

Would I ever be able to go down that road? Even drive it with Mom? What if she was wrong? What if I would never be strong enough to go Out There, even with her. I'd done it last night. But only by accident. Could I do it again? Deliberately? Maybe Page would come, if I asked her.

But then I remembered: Page hated me. Every time she saw me she'd think of this night. And how I'd ruined her life. She'd probably never talk to me again.

CHAPTER THIRTY-TWO

Mom stayed home the next day, calling around about shrinks. She finally set up an appointment with a woman named Marianne Gruber. Mom and I talked a lot, too, and having someone to share my worries with gave me a little bit of hope that I might actually get better. It was weird, but it was as if somehow, by telling someone about them, my fears seemed less terrifying. Dad hung around, too, awkwardly trying to help me relax, until Mom finally dragged him away. After some intense whispered discussion, he took to popping in now and again to smile reassuringly, while working hard at looking cool. He made all three meals — I couldn't remember him cooking anything before. He even fed Victor.

"He keeps asking where his girl is. His little *flower*. I presume that's you?"

I laughed and nodded.

The following day, Mom had to go in for another meeting with Sharon.

"I'll drive your mom to work and pick up a few groceries," Dad said. "It'll get me out of your hair for a while anyway. Unless you want me to stay."

"*No*. You go. I'll be fine."

After they left, I couldn't seem to settle – I had to do something. My eye hadn't swollen very much because of the ice packs and my headache had eased a lot. I dressed, braided my hair, grabbed my keys, and wandered across the hall. Victor cheered my arrival like an enthusiastic greeter at a superstore. A pile of folded canvases had been placed on Lotta's worktable, probably the ones Josh had been trying to steal. I wondered if Harmon had looked at them yet. I'd have to tell him about Lotta and her being famous and all. The angel pattern I'd slipped under the door was lying in the middle of the room. I picked it up and put it on the worktable.

"Whaaat a kid. What a giiiirl!" Victor beamed from behind his cage. Then his voice changed, becoming low and even. "I'm happy you came. Now you can work on my angel."

My hair stood up along my arms. Victor mumbled a pumpkin seed, looking innocent.

"You're wicked," I said. "Oh, yes you are."

He bobbed his head up and down. "Oh yes, oh yes. Mad bad Victor – Victory!"

Even so, I couldn't resist going back to look at the angel. Should I work on it? But if I did, I still wanted to change it – make it brighter, happier, maybe even have the angel's head turned toward the viewer. Somehow help the woman falling through the dark sky. I could sketch it out first.

I studied the pattern. It reminded me of my last 'dream' – that heart-stopping moment when I'd fallen through the glass stairs. Was this how Lotta felt inside? Did she *still* feel this way? How could she? She was dead. She couldn't feel *anything*. I had only imagined her standing beside his cage. Victor spoke in her voice, but it wasn't actually Lotta talking to me.

Was it?

I went through the drawers and cupboards, picking out lighter hues of the colors indicated on the pattern. And then, nervously, I began to sew. Slowly, I grew more confident, blending colors and stitching small sections at a time. It worked. It *did*. The part of the wing I was working on was now bathed in a gentle light. I pulled the pattern over and sketched in a profile of the angel, but I had to stop when my head started to ache from the concentration.

Was I doing the right thing? I mean, what if someone found an unfinished Picasso. Did they have the right to finish it? To change it? I sat down in the armchair by the front window and had just leaned my head back and closed my eyes when the door opened. I figured it would be Harmon, who'd promised to visit me sometime during the day, but instead of a big guy with a plateful of cookies, a slight girl stood in the doorway.

Page.

"Hi." Her hair stood up in damp spikes. One side of her face was a dull swollen red. "I noticed your key in the door so ... okay to come in?"

"Sure."

"Your eye's a beautiful magenta mixed with indigo blue – like a sunset."

"Yours is more like a purple and yellow pansy," I offered.

She smiled. "I've just come to – to tell you … I went to see Dr. Waltron yesterday, that shrink I talked to you about? I told her what happened, and she said you were willing to risk your own safety for me – and that's the sign of a real friend. Unlike Josh. But she'd always said Josh wasn't a friend. I didn't want to believe her." She perched on the edge of a wooden chair. "I'm sorry, Addy."

"Me too."

"For what?"

"About Josh. About being the cause of him leaving."

"You weren't the cause. *He* was."

I whispered. "The thing is, I knew what he was … doing to you … but I kind of just ignored it."

"What could you have done? Look at me. Ms. Independent, right? Harmon asked me once if Josh hit me. I got really mad at him, so he laid off, but he kept hinting that I should dump Josh. And a few times, when Josh got rough, I was going to. But he's always so sorry afterward, and I'd remember how nice he could be and … I'd forgive him."

"So he wasn't always … like he was on Friday?"

She shook her head. "It's as if he had this split personality or something, you know?"

I pointed at the canvases. "Was he really going to sell them?"

"Yeah. I told him that people would be suspicious about where he got them, but he said that any gallery would buy them. He'd just say he was Lotta's nephew."

"How did he get in here?"

"My fault. I was so stupid. I told him what you told me about her work — because it was so interesting. So he hung around Sean and just took Harmon's key from the kitchen. He even brought the pieces up to show me. Can you believe it? He said the money would set us up in Toronto. When I told him what an idiot he was being, he said he'd put them back if I gave him the guitar. But no way. I wouldn't do it. So he just walked out. I kept trying to stop him, but ... that's when he exploded."

"Bet he didn't expect me, huh?"

"I'm sorry about your eye — you could have been really hurt."

"Forget it," I said firmly. "It wasn't *your* fault."

Silence curled around us for a few minutes. I picked up a piece of silk thread stuck to my sweater and stroked its gleaming softness. Page looked out the window.

"I guess I'm never going to see him again," she whispered. "It's hard to take it all in. He's calling all the time. Threatening. Yelling. Pleading. Harmon can't be on guard twenty-four hours a day, but he and Sean have got it all worked out in case Josh shows up. Harmon's a great guy."

And Dad thinks he's taking Mom away from him, I wanted to add, but didn't. "Are you afraid that Josh — that he'll come back?"

She shrugged. "Harmon's pretty worried."

"Will Josh stay in Winnipeg?"

She shook her head. "When he called the last time he said he was going to Toronto with the guys. He wanted me to come. I said no. He got pretty ugly about it, so I hung up. Then Harmon loaned me his answering machine. Josh left three messages. It's like he's lost it completely. But it's hard – I don't know what I'll do if he keeps begging me to come with him." She looked at her chewed fingernails. "I don't expect people to understand, but I still love him, you know? We went through a lot together. I know he has ... problems. But I also know I can't go back –"

A small clatter came from behind us. "Good riddance. Bad rubbish – rid the rubbish –" the last word ended in a strangled croak.

"Is that why you stayed with him ... through everything? Because you loved him?"

She gazed out the window and chewed her thumbnail. "I've never had anyone that was just for me, you know? Except Gramps. I thought Josh would be there forever. *Love*. Pathetic, eh?"

"No. Not pathetic," I whispered. "I think I know how you feel." We were silent for a few minutes, then, "I can't leave the house by myself anymore. Mom thinks it's something called agoraphobia."

She nodded. "Yeah. I figured."

"You did?"

"Yeah."

"I don't know if I can ... do it. Leave. Ever."

She leaned close and whispered, "Yes you can. I told you — you're stronger than you think. But you know that, right?"

I nodded, unable to speak.

"You can do it — and so can I," she said in a firm voice.

Her clear gaze searched my face, then she reached over and took my hand and slid her fingers through mine until our palms touched. We sat like that for a long time. Finally she gently released my hand and walked out the door.

A few minutes later I got up to leave. I was shutting the door behind me when a voice whispered, "Don't leave. Stay here with —"

A shiver skittered through me and I quickly closed the door.

CHAPTER THIRTY-THREE

For dinner we ate chicken wings and a caesar salad that Dad had bought at a local deli. No conversation, just the clink of knives and forks. I tried not to think about the voice that had whispered, "Don't leave. Stay …" Just Victor acting up. Wasn't it?

Finally, Mom wiped her mouth with a paper napkin, flicked a quick glance at Dad, and said, "Your father's decided to go back to Toronto tomorrow."

I stared at him. "I thought you were staying a few more days."

"I got a call from work. One of my biggest commercial customers is coming to Toronto." He pushed at his salad with his fork. "Your mom says you two have figured out how to get the help you need. I think it's best if I go, kiddo. I'm not needed here – I've just loused things up anyway."

"That's not true, Wally," Mom said. "We were able to sort this out as a family – together. Right, Addy?"

I nodded. A jab of anger ran through me. He couldn't even stay the short time he'd promised.

Dad was waiting for me to say something. Mom smiled at me sadly, as if to send me a message, but there was nothing more to say. He'd made his decision.

The phone rang while we were doing the dishes.

I covered the receiver with my hand. "Page wants me to go upstairs for a little while tonight. Is that okay?"

Mom gave me a warning look. Dad just kept drying the same dish, over and over.

I said to Page, "I can't. It's my dad's last night here. Mom's working at the pub later on, so I'm going to spend some time with Dad."

When I hung up, he murmured, "Don't stay home on my account. I'll be gone tomorrow."

"Oh, Dad, come on." I was still mad, but I also felt a twist of guilt. I couldn't let him know I was actually looking forward to him not being around – bugging Mom, fussing over me, making things worse. I tried to make it a bit better. "I just forgot for a second, okay? No big deal. Honest."

He shrugged one shoulder and continued to shine the plate.

"I'm catching a lift with Harmon tonight, in case you need the car, Wally," Mom said, grabbing her coat. "You and Addy might want to rent a movie or something. I won't be late. See you later."

I took the plate out of Dad's hand and put it away, then tipped the water out of the drain board and put it under the sink.

"So, what do you want to do tonight?" I asked, hating my dull voice and wishing I could escape upstairs.

"Shall I get us a video?" he asked.

"If you want."

"I could run your mom to work and pick one up on the way back." He rushed out of the kitchen. "If I can catch her."

A few minutes later, he was back.

"She moved fast enough," he said bitterly. "She didn't need to go with him. It *is* my last night here."

"Why shouldn't she go with Harmon? They're both going to the pub," I said. "Besides, it's not like you'll be around next week to organize her life. Or mine."

I regretted my words instantly. Please don't let me ruin his last night here, I whispered to the silent room. I sat on the living-room couch, and he took the chair across from me. His eyelids had reddened, as if near to tears. That couldn't be possible. Not the high-rolling real estate agent of the universe Walter Jarrick.

"Addy." He linked his fingers together and lowered his head, examining the tips of his shoes. "I know I haven't made things easy for you and your mom. But it hasn't been easy for me, either. I'm not looking to make excuses. It's just that ... I worry about you. I miss you."

I took a deep breath. "Then why blame Mom for everything?"

He glanced up at me in surprise. "Your mom and I have done some talking. I think I've accepted my share of any blame that's going around."

"But *why* does it always have to be about blame?"

"I don't know," he murmured. "I guess when she took the job here I felt that all the sacrifices I'd made over the years weren't worth anything. She just assumed I'd pull up stakes and follow her. And I couldn't. I was so hurt, I just withdrew – from everything – let her go …" He shook his head. "I thought she'd be back by Christmas, but that won't be happening. It's all coming down around me."

"Maybe you hoped –" I stopped.

"Hoped what?"

"Maybe you were really hoping she would take this job – that she'd go away and you could stay behind – and that would end the marriage thing."

He was silent for a few seconds, then murmured, "I don't honestly know, Addy."

"Yes, you do."

He sighed. "We haven't been hitting it off for a while. But we were hanging in there. Then she took Sharon's job offer and …" He shook his head. "Look how you're living! I can't believe she's happy here. And that guy downstairs – God!"

"This is about our family. You and me and Mom. *Okay?*"

He nodded. "Yeah. You're right." He walked over to the window. "I always thought if I did everything by the book – and did it well – that things would work out. There was always this tension between your mom and me. Lately, it got worse … she's never understood how important my work is to me –" He stopped.

"You never had very much time for Mom and me, did you? Work came first."

"That's not fair, Addy. Everything I've done has been for you."

"So, if work's so important, why did you ever agree to come here — and then back out?"

He gazed out the window, his hands in his pockets, his shoulders slumped. "Your mother has always been fearless when it comes to trying new things. I'm different. I've always been afraid to take chances outside of my work — never liked risk, change." He looked down at his shoes and sighed. "I think I got caught up in the romance of it — changing one's life completely, taking that Big Risk. But I just couldn't do it in the end."

"Maybe you were like me — afraid of going to places you were unsure of, afraid to go *out there*."

He sighed again. "Honey, I don't think there's any comparison here, okay?"

"Isn't there, Dad? I mean, it's just a *job*. How can it be your whole life?"

He was silent for a long time. Finally, he sat on the coffee table and took my hands in his. "You think I've been hiding away all these years? Safe inside my work? Afraid to ... *live*?" he asked.

"Maybe ... something like that. Can't you even think about coming here one day?"

He looked sad. "I don't think I can change things now, Addy, even if I wanted to. Not the way things are between me and your mom. I wish you'd come home with me."

"I've got to stay here, Dad. With her."

He nodded. "I know, kiddo. And I won't make things harder for you." He ran his hand over my head. "It'll take guts for you to go out there, but you'll do it. I know you will, when it's time."

I nodded. I knew then that I'd have to take some of those Big Risks. I couldn't lock myself away. Not like Dad. Not like Lotta.

"I'll start small, but I'll start. One small step for girlkind, huh?"

He kissed me on the forehead. "I'll go and get that movie. But I think I'll make it a comedy, okay?"

CHAPTER THIRTY-FOUR

The next morning, Dad finished his packing while Mom got ready for work.

"I've said my good-byes," she said at the door. "I'll bring dinner home." She was being so hearty and cheery it was unnerving.

"Mom? Are you okay?"

"Of course!" she said brightly, then grimaced. "I think so."

"Is Dad?"

"He's okay – but feeling pretty alone, I think. Be kind to him, okay, sweetie?"

"Will you guys ... what are you –"

She pulled a yellow tam over her hair. "We've got lots of talking to do, your dad and me. He set us up on the Internet this week, so we can e-mail each other." She laughed a dry little laugh. "Maybe we'll actually talk – something we haven't done for a long, long time."

"Mom?" I began, but she put one finger on my lips and said, "He's got a lot to think about, Addy, and so do I."

"What about Harmon?"

She leaned over and kissed me. "You ask too many questions. I hope I'll have the answers soon, honey. Give us all some time, okay?"

"As long as I get some, too."

"We've got time enough for everything."

As soon as the door clacked shut behind her, Dad crept out of hiding.

"Cab should be here any minute," he said.

"You want me to walk you downstairs?"

"No. I'll go now and … wait outside."

He buttoned his coat and tied a wool scarf around his neck. We stood awkwardly, not looking at each other. Then he put down his bag and gave me a hard, tight hug. "You'll answer the phone now without banging it in my ear I hope, yeah?" His voice was thick.

I nodded vigorously into his jacket. It smelled of wool and aftershave. Suddenly I didn't want him to go. I held on tight.

He gently loosened my arms and looked at my face as if he wanted to memorize every single molecule of it.

"You know how to use e-mail?"

"Yeah, we learned at school," I whispered, not trusting myself to speak out loud.

"Good. Write me every day. Even just a few lines. Promise?"

I nodded again.

He picked up his bag, opened the door and was gone.

I waited at the window until his cab arrived. Before getting in, he looked up over the roof of the car and waved. I waved back and didn't move until the cab swerved around the corner, throwing up an arc of slush.

I sent a promise after him to write every day.

I knew this would never be his home. He'd never be comfortable in the new life Mom and I had. A knot behind my eyes dissolved into tears of sadness and longing for the way things might have been. But at least we'd never be strangers again. And that was good.

Just below me, two figures walked down the front path toward the street. My heart stopped, then began pumping again when I realized it wasn't Josh with Page, but Sean. I hesitated, then shoved open the window. "Hey! Where are you guys going?"

"To get a video for tonight," Page called up. "There's a new Monday night classic special at Bijou Video. I was going to call you later, after your dad left, to see if you wanted to watch."

"How about my place?" I asked.

"You got popcorn, I hope?" Sean said.

I nodded.

"So what kind of flick do you like?" he asked. "Ginger Roberts and Fred Astaire?"

"Ginger Rogers — *not* Roberts," I laughed. "Anything. I like anything."

"Yikes! don't say that," Page yelped. "You know what guys are like!"

"You decide then, Page."

Sean looked at me and then at Page and back at me again. "Not all guys like blood and guts, stalker, nuclear war blitzes, you know. I like Ginger *Rogers* as much as the next ... uh ... guy."

Page patted his arm. "Right, Sean. We'll be there about eight, okay, Addy?"

"Okay."

She squelched down the path, leaving Sean standing there, head still cocked toward me.

"Need anything at the store?" he called.

"Not this morning."

"I'll see you later?" he asked, as if reluctant to go.

"Sean. Come on. You'll have lots of time to spend with Addy tonight," Page shouted.

He turned so quickly that he slid on a patch of icy snow and almost fell. He righted himself with great dignity and ignored Page's hoots of laughter. They pushed and shoved each other down the street. Something burst inside me – something so old and strangely familiar it almost scared me.

I was happy.

I was so unnerved by the thought that I started to search for something to make me miserable again – to get a jump on those terrors that would try to stamp out this tiny glow inside me and turn it to something cold and fearsome.

No.

I was going to enjoy this old remembered emotion – this desire to turn on loud music and dance. Energy sizzled right into my toes. I flew down the hall, yanked on my sneakers, and went in search of Lotta's angel. I could sew for hours.

CHAPTER THIRTY-FIVE

I'd thought about the angel a lot. I'd been happy with my first changes, so I decided I'd take another look and decide what to do next.

Victor didn't say a word when I walked in.

"What's up?" I asked him.

He rolled his eyes and muttered, "Biiiig trouble."

What was he talking about now? I walked to the angel. All the colors and stitches I'd put in had been taken out. The cut threads were in a little pile on the table. "Who did this?" I cried. "Why?"

"Not what she wanted," Victor moaned. "She not happy!"

"Who? Lotta? Come on, Victor!"

He looked at me, head down, eyes never wavering. "It is not your work. It is my work," he said in Lotta's voice.

"Well, do it yourself then!" I shouted. "I can't do it your way. It's too sad — too dark and unhappy."

The woman's voice was clear and strong. "I insist you do it. You must stay and finish it."

Something moved near Victor's cage. I closed my eyes tight, certain she was in the room.

"You must do it," she continued. "You have the skill."

"Skill? I can do nice stitches, right? You want me to stay locked up in here so your precious picture gets done? Well, I won't."

"I have no hope ... other than you," said the voice. "You must help me do this."

"If you can take the stitches out, why can't you put them back in? You don't need me."

"Yes, I do. But you want to make it yours. You can't. It's mine. Do it."

"Do it yourself then!" I cried, glaring around the room. "I'm not your prisoner. I'll do my own designs. *I'm not you.* Leave me alone. Why don't you take it and go away?"

"I can't – can't go ... not *out there*. This is the only safe place I've known. The angels always told me what to do. All my life. Then one day they stopped. Everyone I cared about was gone. That's when I knew that to survive, I had to stay here. And I wanted to survive despite everything. Staying here is *my* choice. I won't go. And you *must* stay, too!"

This couldn't be happening. I had been so happy, and now she was dripping her misery all over me. "You aren't even here! How can you decide to stay or leave? You're dead. I'll *make* you go away!"

I grabbed as many of the canvases as I could, ran downstairs with them, and hammered on Harmon's door. I don't know if my hair was on end or what but he grabbed the pile of canvases and led me into his apartment. "What's up? What's this load of stuff, kiddo?"

"Don't call me that!" I snapped. "That's what my dad calls me."

He nodded slowly. "Okay. What can I do for you, Addy?"

"You have to figure out what to do with her work. There's so much of it. I don't want the responsibility, I just want that room cleared out. I'll bring it all down. I shouldn't have to take care of her things!"

He unrolled one of the tapestries – the one with the little angel flying through the air on a dragonfly. "Wow. Are they all this beautiful? I was so busy that night I didn't really look at them."

I nodded, keeping my tone even despite my shaking heart. "All of them. There's hundreds of designs. I can't look after them. I won't!"

He nodded. "Okay. We'll move them into my bedroom, and I'll get onto someone who will look them over and tell me how to preserve them. Then we'll know what to do with them."

"You can't sell them!"

"I didn't say anything –" he began.

"She wouldn't like that! But I – I won't look after them for her ... I *can't!*" I closed my mouth tight when I realized I was wailing.

"I won't sell them before discussing it with you, okay? Maybe we can donate them to the art gallery. We'll work something out. Come on, let's go get them out of there."

It took us about half an hour to gather up the tapestries. The whole time I peered furtively around – not daring to even look at Victor, who was utterly silent.

"What about this one?" Harmon pointed at the unfinished angel.

Victor made a little sobbing noise.

"No," I said impulsively, "I'd like to keep that one here."

"Want to come down and have some tea?" Harmon asked. "I don't know about you, but my throat's dry."

I felt hollow and drained. "No. I've got schoolwork to do."

"Well ... you know where I am." He patted my cheek and left.

I stood in the middle of the room. It didn't look much different, yet it felt terribly empty – and so did I. Was she gone? Harmon had insisted I keep all the supplies. The room was mine now. Could I use it? I took the angel off the frame, folded all the dark threads inside it, and stuffed it in Lotta's desk. Then I pulled the top shut. The angel would never ever be finished.

When I closed the door behind me, Victor didn't say a word. I stood in the hallway feeling as if I'd lit a match in my stomach.

What had I done?

CHAPTER THIRTY-SIX

That night I popped a huge bowl of popcorn while Sean gave me culinary advice about dry popping versus oil popping. I think I answered in a fairly intelligent way, because he didn't look at me as if I was speaking gobbledygook, but my thoughts were flying in all directions. I hadn't actually talked to a ghost, had I, like Gene Tierney did in *The Ghost and Mrs. Muir?* And if I had talked to a ghost, was she gone now? If she was all in my head, would I ever get rid of her?

I think I laughed in all the right places in the new Tom Hanks movie, but I couldn't have told you the plot if my life depended on it. And I'm a huge Tom Hanks fan. When it was over, I decided to tell them what I'd done with Lotta's tapestries, just to see if it would sound as awful as I felt.

Sean said, "I think you did the right thing, especially if they're worth a lot of money. I've already suggested that a nice little car would be good," he added, grinning.

"They're Lotta's. They belong together. You can't sell them off!"

"Okay, okay … jeez … Pop will do the right thing by them. I bet he talks it over with you, and me, and anyone

229

else who'll listen – about a hundred times each – before he decides."

I could feel panic deep inside my chest. "I should have left them in the room. She won't like it. She'll be so angry!"

"Who will be angry, Addy?" Page asked.

"I just want to make sure that they're properly taken care of, that's all." I shook my head. "Look, I'm really tired, okay? I gotta get to bed. My mom will be home soon, and I promised I'd crash early."

They both stood up. Page asked, "You okay, Addy?"

"Yeah. Sure. Why wouldn't I be? I'm still … my head hurts when I get tired, that's all."

"Right. Well, see you. Maybe you guys'll come up to my place tomorrow and …"

I nodded even though I wasn't sure what she'd actually said.

Sean looked pleased. "Sounds great," he said. "And how about a hot game of rummy?"

When he walked past me, Sean rested one finger on my shoulder and looked into my eyes. I tried to smile, but it turned into a pathetic quivery thing. I closed the door quickly after them.

The apartment was suddenly cold and very empty. Why had I rushed them away? I got a glass of water, put a CD in the player, and curled up on the couch under Mom's comforter. I lay there thinking about Lotta. I'd taken away everything she loved. Was she gone now? Could someone actually "kill" a ghost? Could I ever work in that room again?

She said she wouldn't go. She said I had to do the

design. That I had to stay. But she'd actually removed the stitches I'd put into her angel's wings, hadn't she? So why couldn't she do the work herself? Why did she really want me to stay? Was she lonely? Did this mean I'd have to give up sewing? I'd loved working on the angel. I'd loved choosing the colors … so many colors …

Slowly the angel design rose in front of me. I lifted a heavy hand and began to count the stitches I'd carefully put into its wing.

I got up and opened the door. The long hallway with the colored doors shimmered into view. I reached into my pocket and pulled out a single red thread. When I opened the red door, there she was … standing near the window of the studio. She wasn't the young woman in the mental hospital. She looked a bit older than Mom, with strands of silver in her straight black hair. She wore soft wide-legged brown trousers and a man's white shirt, the sleeves rolled up past her elbows. On her feet was a pair of old basketball sneakers. No makeup. No jewelry. She took two steps toward me, her thin face acknowledging that she recognized me.

"I can get them back!" I cried. "I'm sorry!"

She shook her head. "No. You did the right thing. They must be cared for if they're to survive. I like that man. He'll be good to them. They'll be yours one day. I can see it." She looked at me intently. "Tell me now … will you do the last angel for me?"

"I can't. It's not mine. I want to do my own work. You have to do it."

She shook her head. "I can't."

"But why? If you can take stitches out why can't you put them in?"

"I wanted to finish it before … before I passed to this place. But the unforgivable happened. You see, I began to *enjoy* working on this last angel. That wasn't allowed. I wanted to show how the angels had turned their backs on me. How they'd let me fall into madness alone. I wanted to punish them. But slowly I felt myself moving closer to them again. Such a struggle. Then, one day, someone came to my front door. I went to answer it … and a dark angel appeared behind me … pushed me – to keep me from finishing it."

"But it wasn't an angel – it had to be Victor who flew up behind you. You *can* finish it. You must!"

She looked startled. "No – I was finally punished. For not warning my family."

"But it wasn't your fault. How could it be! You didn't cause the accident that killed them! And I'm sure it *was* Victor at the stairs. That was just an accident, too! None of it was your fault. None!"

Slowly she shook her head – and began to fade away.

I tried to call her back. "Lotta, listen. It wasn't the angels' fault. It wasn't your fault – or even Victor's … it just happened!" But my words seemed to fly away on an icy blast of wind.

I woke up suddenly, knowing exactly what I had to do – otherwise nothing would change.

CHAPTER THIRTY-SEVEN

The next morning, as soon as Mom left for work, I went straight into the studio, pulled open the blinds and, with a lot of cursing, opened all the windows a crack, letting in the cool, crisp air. Sunlight flooded the room. I left both doors open so I could walk between my apartment and the studio. Might as well, seeing as how it was all one apartment now.

Victor watched in silence while I set up one of Lotta's extra sewing frames and rolled on a new piece of penelope canvas. I laid down a tracing pad, a pile of colored pens and some graph paper, ready for my new design. Then I opened the desk, pulled out the angel tapestry, and rewound it onto Lotta's frame, putting all the colors she'd chosen beside it, along with the pear-shaped pincushion bristling with needles.

"Now, for you," I said to the black eyes watching my every move.

I marched straight at Victor. He backed away and bobbed his shaggy head and tail frantically. "I'm a good boy!" he whispered. "I'm a very very good boy."

"Yes, you are!" I said. "And I love you a lot, you mangy old thing. You didn't mean to hurt Lotta. I know that."

He perked up. "Good boy, Victor. Pretty Victor! Right? Right?"

"That's right. And that's why I've decided –" I lifted my hand. He squawked and fell onto the floor of his cage. "– to keep this open when I'm around. You can have the run of the place as of ... now."

He lifted his head. "Not go out today ... maybe 'nother day."

"I know exactly how you feel." I spoke to the room in general. "And now I'm going to start something new. Something that is *mine*."

I started a drawing of Victor the Bad. He preened himself, looking terribly important, showing me first his left battered side, then his right, and then his half-eaten red tail. First I drew his basic outline, trying to keep it simple, like Lotta suggested in her book – then I began the details. My back was stiff when I finished. I held it up. Looked like him. Maybe his neck was a bit too fat.

"Whhhat a beaaauutiful boy!" he crowed.

I stretched. "Yeah, I'll even put in your missing feathers. But I'm not sure if the gray should be blue-gray or green-gray."

I held swatches of color near his feathers. He tried to grab them, almost falling out the door once, then scrambling back inside with a yelp. I yawned. My eyes hurt and I was hungry. "I'll be right back, Victor. I'm just going for an apple."

"Apple-pan dowdy! Me too. Me too, apple of my eye!" Victor shouted from his cage as I left. "I no fly by. Oooh nooo!"

When I got back, I gave him a nice big piece of apple. I cruised by the frame with Lotta's angel on it. Everything lay exactly as I'd left it. Well, it was only the first day. I sat down to look at my own design and felt the hair on the back of my neck lift. Someone had taken the dark blue pencil and carefully resketched Victor's neck. It looked exactly like Victor now. Beside the design lay five different blue-gray bundles of thread.

"I knew you'd be bossy," I muttered. "But you're right. Thanks."

No one answered. But it didn't matter.

CHAPTER THIRTY-EIGHT

I wish I could say that all of my fears vanished into the fresh air and sunshine in the studio that day – that I discovered I could go Out There any time I felt like, without that metallic taste of panic in my mouth. I wish I could say that Dad flew back a few days later and manfully strode in announcing he'd come to live with us forever.

I wish I could. But I can't.

Dad's still in Toronto. I write him short notes every evening, to tell him how my day went and to let him know how I'm getting along with the psychologist. It's been four months since I saw him, but he's promised to visit in the spring.

Their divorce is going through. I guess I always thought of Mom and Dad as one being – forever joined together, like the stars and the moon. But they aren't, they're two separate people who can't seem to make each other happy. In a funny way, I think we work better as a family when they're apart. Dad's dating – believe it or not, he's actually going out with Mrs. Perdaski's daughter Rosa, who's a school librarian. Dad says she likes his house and all the old things in it.

That's okay with me. I don't think of the house as *ours* anymore. He says he's kept my room the same for me though – for when I feel able to travel to Toronto. When I told Mom Dad's news, she looked sad for a while, but then she smiled. "Well, maybe this time it'll work out for him. I hope so."

Mom and Harmon see each other all the time, and I think they'll stay together. She seems happy in her work and is my number one "safe person." That's what my doctor, Marianne Gruber, calls the person who stays with you every single second when you venture Out There. Harmon is my second safe person. I've forgiven him for loving Mom, and I know he really cares about me, too. But the best part is, I've never seen Mom this happy. I didn't know she could be so full of laughter.

Page is staying in school. Harmon co-signed her student loan, and I know she won't let him down. She hasn't heard from Josh in ages. She works a lot at the pub to pay her loan back, but we see each other often. I think I've finally made a real friend. I got a second letter from Jodie, wondering if something was wrong and asking why I hadn't written. I think, maybe, I'll write her back. Can't hurt … right?

I work every day for a few hours on my sewing, with Victor yakking away at me. Mom and I moved the dining-room set into our living area and my bedroom furniture in to the studio, so the studio feels like my own special place now – well, three-quarters mine, anyway.

I'm slowly reading all of Lotta's books, and I've finished two of my own designs. They're nowhere near as good as

Lotta's, but I like them. Right now I'm designing my own tree. I'll leave two of the panels empty, so I can fill them in when I'm older. I have one dark panel – kind of like Lotta's angel behind bars – except it's me standing in a dark hallway in front of a door covered in padlocks. I'm slowly working on my next one. In it, I've used a big gold key to open the door. I'm still partially standing in shadow, but behind the open door are all the vivid rich colors I see when I manage to go Out There. This small square is a mix of light and dark colors. Kind of like real life, I guess. I'm hoping my next one will be brighter, but who knows? Life can never be full sunshine all the time, can it?

I'm able to go to some places Out There now, as long as either Mom or Harmon is with me – safe places like a quick walk in the park or a car ride around the neighborhood.

It's taken a lot longer to go out on my own, but I've done it. Once. To the door of Nucci's grocery and back – with Mom, wrapped in scarves and woolies, waiting for me by the front gate. Tomorrow my goal is to go inside the little store on my own and buy a chocolate bar. Sean's going to meet me there. It's what Marianne told me to do. Plan ahead. Work toward a goal. Make it fun. Give yourself a reward.

Marianne says that now I've finally accepted that I have this problem, I will get better much faster. But she also warned me not to get discouraged. "No overnight cures" and "One goal at a time" are her favorite phrases.

One of my big goals is to go to a movie with Sean and Page. It may take awhile, but I'll do it.

The other day, Harmon told me that a fabric expert will be coming over next week to tell us how to protect Lotta's work. And that the Griffin Gallery would love to have a show of her angels. He's decided he won't sell any of them, but loan them out to various galleries around the country.

As for Lotta, well, things have inched forward a bit. She's certainly keeping busy – advising me, leaving little hints all over the place. And then, a few days ago, when I went into the studio, the paper design for her angel was open on the table. Some of the colors had been changed, and I think she's redesigning parts of it, too. But since then the page has vanished. I wonder what she's doing to it? I hope I find out soon.

One thing is sure – I'm not afraid of her anymore. I feel separate from her, but I also understand why she ended up so unhappy. I won't let that happen to me. And I think, in time – maybe by watching me – she'll finally feel able to go Out There on her own, too.

Last night I dreamed again that I was falling. I stood on the edge of a tall building and closed my eyes and leaned forward into the wind. Then I let myself go. Down, down I fell until I could feel the familiar scream of panic in my chest. But then, with a swoosh of wings, someone caught me – held me for the briefest moment – and let me go.

But I didn't keep falling. This time, I opened my arms and I flew.